A Kiss in the Rain

NANCY LOYAN

ISBN # 978-0-9861900-3-2

Interior format by The Killion Group
http://thekilliongroupinc.com

DEDICATED TO:

The Chautauqua Institution

ACKNOWLEDGEMENTS

The esteemed Chautauqua Institution in Chautauqua, New York is close to my heart for many reasons. I was introduced to the Institution by a friend at church, who suggested that I send them a proposal to instruct a dance class for their Special Studies program during the nine-week "Season." I sent in a proposal that was accepted. I had never been to Chautauqua and didn't know what to expect.

When I entered the gates, it felt as if I were coming home and my smile remained the entire week until it was time to leave, when my eyes filled with tears. The Chautauqua Institution is not so much a place, but an experience. You either "get it" or you don't. It is considered the "intellectual's paradise" or "Disneyland for nerds."

For nine weeks during the summer, this sleepy Victorian village awakens like the mythical Brigadoon to fuel the mind, body and spirit. The famous from politics and academia lecture, renowned ministers preach and entertainers perform. The Institution has its own symphony and youth orchestras, ballet, opera and theater companies. Located on scenic Chautauqua Lake, numerous recreational activities abound for adults and children, from sailing, kayaking, canoeing, swimming and more. There is even a Steamboat, the Chautauqua Belle that picks up passengers from the Institution for an historic lake tour. The Institution hearkens back to America's past with a patriotic, old-fashioned, wholesome, friendly and safe environment.

Founded as a summer Methodist retreat for ministers and Sunday school teachers, the Institution maintains its religious roots by honoring the Abrahamic faiths: Christian, Jewish and Muslim. Denominational houses offer affordable lodging. There are quaint inns, condominiums and houses for rent and the elegant and historic Athenaeum Hotel.

I am honored and privileged to have been selected as a Special Studies instructor in dance and writing.

For years, I have taken notes with the thought of incorporating my favorite place in America as the location of a novel. I did take some literary license, however. I just hope that this novel, though a romantic suspense and not a literary work, does the Chautauqua Institution justice.

There are so many people to thank and honor that I fear that I would leave someone out. Let's just say that the Special Studies department, the administration, staff, and employees of the Institution are an amazing group of individuals. To the innkeepers I have resided with and the friends that I've made, I love all of you and cherish the memories.

I would be remiss if I did not acknowledge some special friends for their inspiration: Janet, Rick, Stephanie, Jason and Julie at the Tally Ho for their care, Harriett Culp for her guidance and Jim Roselle for his radio show. Bonnie Rosenthal, Barbara Friedman, Dennis Wolrod, Jolie McShane, Judy and BLA for their friendship. Special thanks to Darlene Westfall at the Sweet Spot Café for her muffins, and Jeannie at the Mayville Diner for the pancakes. I'd also like to thank Matt at The Chautauqua Belle for the memories. Thank you, Janet Fitchko, for the editing help.

This book wouldn't be as special if not for Steven Novak's wonderful cover art and Jennifer at The Killion Group, Inc. for her dedication and care to its layout. To my Crimson CR Sisters, especially Deborah O'Neill Cordes…

I love you!!!

Sometimes you have to know where you came from to know where you are going...

CHAPTER 1

Damn him! Damn him for coming back into town and for coming back into her life. At least twenty years had passed and enough water had gone over the bridge to sink a fleet of battleships.

Darrin Carter swaggered into her lobby like he owned the place. Actually, he could have if life circumstances had gone as planned. After all, he was the son of innkeepers. She was the last person to have ever imagined owning and operating an inn, especially at the Chautauqua Institution. She recalled the famous aphorism by the late John Lennon, "Life is what happens to you while you're busy making other plans."

Darrin looked too good. Gone was the shy, gangly, awkward, and nerdy boy. He had morphed into an athletically built, confident, and handsome man. His face had lost its baby fat and was all planes and angles, with high cheekbones and a square jaw. His hair was just as dark as she had remembered but the curls had been trimmed short. The only things that remained the same were his dimpled smile, and those deep green eyes. They had probably melted and broken many hearts.

"Katherine?" he asked when his gaze met hers. It was more deer-in-the-headlights than a familiar greeting.

She had looked up from the leather-bound guest register book she had been pretending to peruse when he entered, scoping him out from the corner of her eye. She was so startled, she was rendered speechless.

"Katherine Morrow?" he repeated.

All she could manage was a nod.

She was surprised when he had recognized her. She had changed. The straight and skinny girl had grown into hourglass curves, her pale blonde hair into amber curls, and her designer wardrobe reduced to worn jeans and tee shirts. Too bad that he recognized her. The memories that his surprise appearance conjured up were more nightmare than nostalgia.

"I can't believe it's you. I can't believe you're here, of all places."

She wanted to crawl into the floorboards and disappear. How many times had she dreamed about him, wondering how he was, where he was, when and if their paths would ever cross. This was not the reunion she had in mind. Not now. Not here. *Never here.*

"Katy, what are you doing here?" He leaned on the sturdy oak counter, his gaze unwavering, as potent as ever.

Hell if she knew. Why did he have to call her by the nickname he had given her so many years ago, the only person ever to use it?

"I own and manage this inn," she said, watching him tilt his head, questioning.

While her guests enjoyed the amenities of the seasonal, upscale, gated environment, she worked. Long ago, she determined that she didn't owe anyone an explanation. Especially Darrin Carter, now that he returned.

"What are you doing here?" she asked. Right when she thought that she had reconciled with her past and moved on, the one person who had experienced the tragedy had come back like a ghost to haunt her.

Silence.

"I'm here for business. My assistant made the reservation," he replied.

She shuffled through the reservations book. "Oh, I see. That's why your name isn't here."

"It was reserved under Brantley Wentworth."

She perused the entries and pointed to the name and blank space. She turned the book toward him.

"Could you sign in?"

He chuckled. "This place never changes. The inns don't use computers, and I bet you still don't accept credit cards?"

"No."

He removed a fancy gold ballpoint from the pocket of his navy sport coat and signed the book. There was no mistaking his distinct, swirling script. She recalled how as children they worked on perfecting their signatures for when they were rich and famous, with people hounding them for their autographs. It was so long ago. Seeing his penmanship made it feel like yesterday. She shuddered at the memory.

He was left-handed and she couldn't help but notice that he wasn't wearing a wedding ring. She told herself that it didn't matter. The past was in the past, over and done.

"There," he said, sliding the pen back into his pocket.

She stared at the signature. He had signed "Brantley Lawrence Wentworth III."

"I don't understand?" She met his cool gaze.

"It's the name I am to be addressed."

"Business?"

He nodded. She knew better than to pry.

"I'll show you to your room."

He picked up the nylon carry-on bag and computer case he had entered with, and waved his arm. "After you."

She grabbed a brass key from a pegboard and rounded the corner of the reception counter. Standing next to him reminded her of his height. As children, she had always been a few inches taller. Time had changed things. He had to be at least six-foot-four to her five-foot-six.

From the corner of her eye, she caught him sizing her up. Yes, I have boobs now, she thought to herself.

She led him across the small lobby with its worn oriental runner, pale rose wallpaper, and antique brass wall sconces. The floorboards squeaked as they walked.

"There's a library for reading and relaxing," she said, pointing out the walnut paneled room with built-in shelves heaving with books. Worn leather sofas and chairs set on a faded Tabriz rug gave it warmth and character. A jewel-toned stained glass window added color.

He nodded.

"There's a parlor for quiet reflection." Her favorite room, it retained its Victorian elegance with a rose velvet parlor set, rosewood and marble tables, oriental carpet, and valences and draperies of floral brocade. A fireplace with carved mantle and a needlepoint screen added to the ambiance.

"And, here's the dining room and conservatory where morning coffee and breakfast are served," she added, inhaling the lingering scent of cinnamon from her morning's baking.

He peeked into the bright glass-walled, wicker-furnished sunroom. "Most important meal of the day."

After, she led him up the narrow staircase with its smoothly worn banister, carved spindles and matted oriental runner up to the second floor and down the hall.

She fumbled with the key in the tarnished brass lock before opening the paneled oak door. Pushing it open, she drew a deep breath and flagged him inside.

"I've let you the largest suite with a view of the lake since you reserved the entire Season," she explained, showing him the living spaces. The suite was furnished with her best family heirlooms. The salon featured a burgundy brocade-covered Victorian parlor set with coordinating scalloped draperies over the narrow windows.

A fireplace with cast iron mantelpiece with embroidered fire screen was set against a wall.

She hesitated before entering the bedchamber, nerves rattling, a foreboding that never left when she entered what was her parents' bedroom suite. She pointed out the mahogany four-poster bed with fabric-canopied frame and matching bureau, wardrobe, and washstand with washbasin and pitcher. There was also a roll-top desk and chair, and overhead fan. "I don't have air conditioning but this will help along with the lake breezes. There's a private porch with a lake view. The bathroom has been totally remodeled with shower and is behind that door. It's quite modern. No need for the washstand."

"So, tell me, Katy, whatever possessed you to return here?"

When she turned to face him, he stared at her and she fidgeted.

"It's a long story and I'm too stunned to discuss it with you now." She was telling the truth. Did she dare tell him of the rough journey that abruptly led her away, and returned her to Chautauqua?

"We'll have time. I'm not leaving any time soon," he said with a smirk that she found unnerving.

"Why are you here, Darrin? You have more reasons to stay away than me? What business would bring you here?"

"My business. And I'm not to be addressed as Darrin. From now on, I'm Brantley Wentworth. We just met. It's very important. Understand?"

She met his all-too-serious gaze and decided not to push him.

He sighed. "I'm a bit tired and still shocked to see you."

"I guess we're even."

"We always were." He said, surveying the room.

"I hope the suite is to your liking?"

"It'll do."

"Enjoy your visit," she said, handing him the room key. A flash of memory was recalled just by brushing his hand.

She walked out of the room as quickly as her unsteady legs would move her. Darrin still had an unsettling effect on her and it was more than just his change of identity.

CHAPTER 2

Katy Morrow! She was the last person on earth Darrin ever expected to see, especially at the Chautauqua Institution. He didn't anticipate the Honeysuckle Inn to be owned by someone who knew him, a complication he neither expected nor welcomed.

How many years had it been? At least twenty. Yet, he recognized her. How could he forget that sweet, heart-shaped face with the smattering of freckles over the bridge of her nose, the sparkling hazel eyes that glinted emerald and amber, and those lips that seemed to be in a perpetual pout? The lips whose butter-soft touch and taste still remained imprinted in memory.

No other woman had ever stirred up the feelings he had for her. Maybe it was the yearning of his first kiss, his first love. Puppy love, his parents had termed it. To him it seemed like much more.

Returning to the Chautauqua Institution had been difficult enough. Years ago, he vowed never to return. Entering the gates sent chills up his spine, and apprehension through his mind. His job dictated the decision that was made for him, not by him.

The New York City field office of The Federal Bureau of Investigation sent him on this assignment. Special Agent Darrin Franklin Carter, an expert of serial crimes, was to lead an important investigation.

Death waited for no one, and the setting was not a choice, even when the location was the most unexpected in the country. Serial killers had strange choices when it came to selecting their victims and places to perpetuate their crimes.

He thought that enough years had passed to buffer the memories. Being on the grounds hadn't affected him as deeply as he expected until he saw Katy Morrow.

Katy "toothpick" Morrow had grown from a tall, skinny girl into a statuesque woman. Her beauty had refined through the years but a weary worldliness shone in her eyes that concerned him. Gone was her sweet innocence and he feared that it was more than the family tragedy.

He was glad that he had not burdened her with the knowledge that a serial killer was on the loose, and that it was his quest to find the killer before she struck again. He was fairly certain that the suspect was female and was rather glad. Katy would not be in danger, he assured himself.

While planning at his office, he selected the obscure, intimate inn as his headquarters. His cover was the nerdy Brantley Lawrence Wentworth, III, CEO of Wentworth Analytics, lucrative Silicon Valley software start-up. He went to the Institution to lure a spider. Now he had to keep Katy out of the tangled web.

The Chautauqua Institution had insisted that the investigation be conducted discreetly. Though there was cooperation with the Chautauqua Police Department and the Chautauqua County Sheriff's Department, all were under orders to keep it quiet and hidden from the masses. One leak and the financial investment, real estate values, tourism dollars, and squeaky-clean reputation would have tarnished the Institution forever. Reputation was everything.

As it was, no one liked the idea of a major investigation being conducted during the important and lucrative nine-week Season. Six prominent men were dead, either selected from or murdered on the grounds during the height of past

Seasons. The Season was the annual summer event, from June through August when the sleepy Victorian hamlet on scenic Chautauqua Lake in the southwestern corner of New York State awakened like Brigadoon.

Originally a retreat for Methodist Sunday school teachers when founded by minister, Dr. John Heyl Vincent and inventor, Lewis Miller in 1874, the 750-acre village swelled from around 400 year round residents to over 7,500 summer residents and 150,000 guests. For nine weeks during the summer, it opened as a gated educational, cultural, and spiritual enclave. Guests paid admission and entered the gates to experience the "Disneyland for intellectuals," "summer camp for nerds," "university for adults" utopia. Some guests stayed for a few days or a week, while others stayed for the entire Season. It attracted upscale, mostly liberal-leaning, curiosity-intellectual seeking educated professionals from around the world. The seasonal gated community with its pricey admission and perceived security provided a family-friendly escape from the real world back into a "Leave it to Beaver" tranquility of the 1950's.

Security. Safety. The wholesome atmosphere was as much a draw as the world-class speakers and entertainers who graced the stage of the famous amphitheater every day and night. Presidents, statesmen, noted journalists, experts, and performers lectured and entertained. Weekly, thought-provoking themes brought discussion and discourse with a mixture of religious beliefs, and collaboration that created a unique atmosphere.

The Chautauqua Institution wasn't a place to be visited, but a special place to be experienced.

As a child, Darrin had taken it for granted. Through the years, friends and acquaintances had lauded it. He felt cheated.

He unpacked his bag, folding his clothes in the bureau, hanging his jackets in the wardrobe, and placing his toiletries in the tiled bathroom. The suite was a bit too cute and feminine for his taste, and a familiar musty scent lingered in the air. It reminded him of his family's inn, where he had been born and raised.

The Carter Inn had been one of the oldest on the Institution grounds. Though it was not located on the lake, it boasted Victorian ambiance with its scalloped trim, turret room, and multiple tiered porches. The rooms were smaller than his suite with sinks in each room and shared bathrooms, modern conveniences added late in its history. The brass light fixtures had been converted from gas to electric shortly after The Athenaeum Hotel, the first commercial electric building in the country. Thomas Edison had married one of the Institution's founder's daughters. Stories about Edison had been passed down through generations of his family just as the inn had been passed down.

His family tree had gone back to the Institution's founding. Through heritage, he should have been the proprietor of a huge, successful inn on the Institution's manicured grounds. Instead, he was the lead investigator on a grizzly murder case where the suspect preyed on victims in one of the safest towns in the nation, the last place one would suspect.

CHAPTER 3

Katherine sat savoring her morning coffee while seated on a swivel stool behind the reception counter. Inn keeping was essentially a twenty-four hour job, especially when you couldn't afford many employees. There were the two part-time Amish housekeepers and the on-call handyman.

Her mind drifted to Darrin. She wondered what kind of business he had at the Institution. It must be important, she surmised, by his serious demeanor. Why did he register under an assumed name? Goosebumps erupted from her wrists up to her shoulders. The last time she felt like this was over twenty years ago. That event, too, involved Darrin.

Of all the inns at the Institution, she wondered why he selected hers. It wasn't just for a few days or a week. He was booked for the entire Season. For nine weeks be would be sleeping in her best suite, eating her Continental breakfasts, and living under her roof. The thought made her jittery and it wasn't the caffeine.

"Good morning."

Speaking of the devil …

Darrin meandered down the stairs and she caught his gaze. She tried her best to remain nonplussed. Inside, though, she was a jumble of nerves. Did the man have to look so good in the morning?

He looked very "Chautauqua-esque" in his khaki cargo shorts, blue tee shirt emblazoned with the CHQ logo, navy baseball cap, and dark tennis shoes. Someone hit the

Chautauqua Book Store for gear. He'd fit in perfectly. What weren't ordinary were his dimpled smile, full lips, and penetrating eyes. The slight growth of beard gave him a devil-may-care attitude that went with his casual stance as he stood in front of her counter.

"Morning," she replied, trying her best to act unaffected. "In the conservatory, you'll find a carafe of coffee, and breakfast fare. I have fresh-baked banana nut bread."

She nodded toward the sunny room but he didn't move. Pretending to appear busy, she shuffled some papers.

"You have a lovely place here. Reminds me of my folks."

She swallowed hard. He had to say that, didn't he?

"Updated to the 21st Century. I do have a computer and printer for guests' use and Wi-Fi as well."

He chuckled. "Thankfully, a few things are modern around here. It's sort of weird, but I feel as if I've been here before."

She watched him scan the surroundings. "Actually, you have been here before."

He met her gaze, questioning.

She swallowed hard. "Before I had it transformed into an inn, this was my parents' summer home."

"This … this belonged to your folks? It looks so different."

She nodded.

"I'll be damned."

"It's the only thing that I inherited," she admitted. "It's all that I have and I've fought hard to keep it."

"Oh, Katy, times have been difficult, haven't they?"

If he only knew.

"It looks like you're doing well now."

"I survive."

The inn was all that she had and every dime she earned went into its upkeep. Every ounce of her energy was devoted to its survival. She lived in it all year to protect it.

The Honeysuckle Inn was her only possession and it possessed her.

"The change is remarkable. I don't remember all the rooms."

"That's what happens when a private home is renovated into an inn with six suites. Some walls were moved, bathrooms were added and there were electrical and plumbing upgrades, not to mention the heating system, fire and security. I'm still paying off the loans." She shrugged her shoulders. "I couldn't afford to keep it as a home, and I often worry that I won't be able to afford to keep it as an inn."

"I can see your determination."

"Disguised as fear."

"No." He smiled. "I think that your ancestors would be proud of you, keeping the family home."

"I don't know. They had it as a sign of privilege. My mother had a Mennonite cleaning lady, a cook, and a gardener. I do most everything myself."

"Hard work has paid off. Don't be so tough on yourself."

"Darrin, … ahh … Mr. Wentworth, I don't need any sympathy. I'm okay."

"Why don't you drink your coffee with me in the conservatory. We can continue our conversation. I would like some company."

"A few other guests are already in there and I'm sure they'd love to chat."

"You used to chastise me about too much work and no play."

"That was in the past."

The past before she lost her childhood, her innocence, her parents, her inheritance, and her future.

"The past is over and done. I've learned to live in the here and now," he said.

She wondered how long that would last, and if returning to Chautauqua would conjure memories better left undisturbed.

"Mr. Wentworth, I hardly know you," she said.

"Ms.? Mrs.?" He asked.

He was prying. "Ms."

He smiled that potent smile.

"Don't get any ideas. The past is over and done, as you said." She turned to the papers, pretending to ignore him.

From the corner of her eye, she saw him begin to speak and stop himself. He turned, and strolled into the dining room.

This was going to be the longest nine weeks on record.

After having coffee, croissants, and banana bread to die for, Darrin went up to his room to review his notes and make some inquiries. The private porch off of his room provided the perfect backdrop for computer work. A slight breeze wafted up from the lake, carrying with it a refreshing freshwater scent. It was a far cry from the exhaust fumes he had grown accustomed to in Manhattan. He drew a deep breath.

He sat on a padded wicker chair at a round wicker table, a perfect spot for his laptop. There was one problem he had not anticipated. The view. The unencumbered view of Lake Chautauqua was breathtaking on this clear and sunny day. Clear days were few and far between, about 20 out of 365 if his recollection was correct. Beyond the Promenade walk and South Lake Drive, the water glistened as if sprinkled with glitter as sailboats with their rainbow-hued sails skimmed across the flowing waves. They were joined by kayakers, and motorboats towing innertubes of squealing children. The steam whistle of The Chautauqua Belle tooted and the historic steamboat came into view with its churning paddlewheel. He half expected a chorus of "Cotton Blossom" from the musical "Showboat" to ring out.

For a moment, he wished that he were Brantley Wentworth III, multimillionaire entrepreneur. He could be enjoying a leisurely vacation among the well-educated, moneyed professionals who were sailing, cycling, playing shuffleboard, ladder ball or bocce on the grounds. Instead, he had work to do. He could bet that he was the only person investigating a heinous crime. Joy.

If the distraction of the view weren't enough, he couldn't stop thinking about Katy. She didn't seem very happy. Her solemn demeanor made him feel guilty. He benefited from the tragedy and she had not. The settlement money funded his college education, M.B.A., law school and led to his becoming a Special Agent. He was raised lovingly by relatives and escaped the past unscathed. It just didn't seem fair that Katy, who was as innocent as he, had suffered for the sins of her father. To top it off, all that she had was the inn. If it had ghosts, it would be haunted.

He wondered what strange fate would have led him to this place, to the inn, to Katy.

Chatting with Darrin was like reopening old wounds and bleeding all over again.

After finishing her coffee, she spent the day as she had every Sunday. It was just another day. There was no time for the ecumenical service in the amphitheater. Just work to be done: baking, cleaning, sorting-washing-folding laundry. Miriam and Sara had the day off and she took over their chambermaid duties as well. Plants needed to be watered and tables dusted. There were guest questions to be answered and problems to be addressed.

The privileged guests at the Institution were jogging the grounds in their designer togs, pushing strollers of cooing babies, walking their pedigreed dogs or sitting on a bench reading novels or thought-provoking diatribes. Many spent the Season in summer homes that were nicer than the permanent residences of most Americans. They were financially stable and comfortable.

She couldn't help but observe the women. Most of them were of average appearance. Few were beautiful or even pretty. Yet, they held hands with handsome husbands who gazed adoringly into their eyes. They had someone to hold them close at night, make love to them, to listen to their troubles, and to share their dreams. She was pretty and smart and she was alone. Alone. She had spent most of her life alone. The way her life was going, she would end it alone as well. She often wondered if she would grow mold and some day just rot while residing at the inn.

Seeing Darrin brought on the pity party. He looked as successful and secure as those husbands. Well, he should. Fate had turned their lives upside down. In his case, he moved up in life. He lived the life she had been entitled to live but had not.

When she observed the sepia-toned photographs adorning the lobby walls, her ancestors stared back. Her maternal great-great grandparents had built the home and it had passed down through the generations. Her mother had called it the family cottage.

It was all she had left of the family legacy. She believed that she owed the previous generation to safeguard it, even if it had to be turned into an inn to assure its survival and lineage.

The house had been in a trust her parents had established at her birth. As an only child, when she turned twenty-one, the deed was handed to her. Only ingenuity and dumb luck kept it in her family. She managed to escape foreclosure and a sheriff's sale. Still awaiting a profit, she barely earned enough to keep the inn, let alone herself, alive.

It was ironic, though, that she would be so nostalgic and yet, not have any children to leave it to. One day it would leave the family and be a legacy lost.

Her mother's memory kept her motivated. The cottage was the only place her mother loved. It was also the one place her father loathed as much as his marriage and his life.

"Excuse me, I'm inquiring about a suite for the Season." The woman's soft, childlike voice startled her from her thoughts.

Katherine met the bespectacled gaze of a petite, forty-something woman. She had the look of a stereotypical librarian with her salt and pepper chin length bob and lack of cosmetics. Peering beyond the counter, she saw the woman's denim jumper, ivory tee shirt, and Birkenstock sandals, and she smiled.

"I'm sorry, but all of my rooms are booked this week. Perhaps, I can suggest another inn?"

"I prefer something quiet."

Katherine chuckled. "The grounds are rather still, especially with quiet time after eleven p.m."

The woman was not amused. "I guess that there's always the Athenaeum."

"Quiet and historical." The grand 1881 Second Empire-style hotel on the grounds would probably suit this mousy, nerdy woman.

The woman perused the lobby, and glanced up the stairs. "I find it interesting how so many women come here alone to seek solitude. It seems that they outnumber the men."

"It may seem that way, but most of my guests are solo men."

"Really?"

The woman's pale face seemed to light up. Maybe she was looking for a date or a mate. The Institution did have its share of couples meeting and marrying on the grounds.

"You know, you can come and visit and sit on the porch if you're in the area," Katherine suggested.

"Thank you. I might just take you up on that offer." The woman winked before turning to leave.

Katherine laughed after the woman left. The woman sought quiet and a man. Funny, how women of all ages were seeking a mate. Everyone except her. She had given up on love years ago. Her adage had become, if it's to be, it's up to me. No man required.

She sighed. There was more work to be done. She had yet to make up the guests' beds and replace their towels with clean ones. She put up a sign on the front desk with her cell phone number and the note to call 911 if it was an emergency. After getting a laundry basket from a storage closet, she began to make her appointed rounds to the guest rooms. Beginning on the first floor, she worked her way upstairs. Everyone had been out and about enjoying the mild, sunny weather. She stood outside of Darrin's door and hesitated. The door was ajar, and she assumed that he had also left. Guests had a habit of leaving doors unlocked. The gated atmosphere lent itself to trust and safety.

She pushed open the door with her foot. Seeing the rumpled bed, she proceeded to straighten and fold the sheets and spread the coverlet. As she was leaning over, she heard someone clear his throat. Startled that Darrin was in the room, she turned her head to catch him staring at her ass. His hand was on his chin, contemplating her. Her face flushed with heat.

"You could have knocked," he said.

"I … I didn't know you were here. Everyone else was gone." She stood, facing him. It seemed strange being alone in a bedroom with him.

"I was out working on the porch."

After placing some clean towels on the bed, she gathered up her basket of dirty linens and towels.

"Looks like I'm not the only one working," he added, approaching her. "Here, let me help you with that."

"Oh, that's not necessary. I'm used to it."

"I thought that you had help."

"I do, except on Sundays when the Amish girls have the day off."

"Do you ever have a day off?"

She stared at him. "Are you kidding? I have an inn to run." She walked toward the door, ignoring his offer.

"Katy, what the hell happened during the past twenty years?"

"I became an innkeeper." She turned and walked out of the room.

CHAPTER 4

"And I became an F.B.I agent," Darrin thought out loud as he sat on the porch, back at work after Katy's abrupt exit.

In his youth, he never imagined himself in law enforcement, yet alone joining the F.B.I. Life circumstances changed his goals. From innkeeper to Special Agent, college and law school with an offer from the F.B.I. that he couldn't refuse.

He leaned back in his chair. There were so many names to research. First, he had employees and volunteers to check, reviewing each resume on file and checking the crime database. Second, he had to research everyone who had purchased a Season pass who had been scanned into the Institution's database, with photographs and demographics recorded. He eliminated men and children from the list, and focused on single women. He wasn't looking for a date. He was looking for a murderess. Somewhere on that list was a "black widow", a woman who preyed on lonely old men, married them in haste, and murdered them for their money or other nefarious reasons. Heaven knows that the Institution had enough lonely, old men. It was no wonder that it had become her location of choice and happy hunting grounds. Fear that she would strike again this Season brought him to the grounds, and he was determined to prevent another tragedy.

He had nine weeks to find and apprehend a serial killer. His past experience and knowledge of the Institution landed him the assignment. Having been trained in psychology and the behavior of serial killers also gave him an edge. The task would not be easy.

The typical "black widow" was a woman seeking vengeance for the violent loss of a loved one: a significant other or husband. Being a serial killer usually involved untreated brain damage. Damage or inactivity of the frontal lobes and temporal lobes were often involved. Impulsiveness, irritability, dysfunction, and violent-aggressive behavior were often combined with Attention Deficit Disorder, creating a dangerous individual without a conscience. Easy to study, difficult to locate. Pouring over names meant little except knowing that one of these individuals was probably his suspect.

He was using himself as a lure by posing as a lonely millionaire in dire need of female companionship. Though younger than the victims' demographic, he surmised that the nerdy money angle would be enough of a lure.

His thoughts kept going back to Katy. He didn't need the distraction. Memories of their youthful past and of her present beauty would only complicate matters. Being under her roof and at the Institution was enough to occupy his mind with thoughts other than business. It was bad enough that she knew who he really was and curious about his alias and reason for being here. This jeopardized his cover.

The ringtone on his cell phone, the theme from Dragnet, interrupted his thoughts.

"Carter," he answered, recognizing the number of the NYC field office.

"Hey, I just received the reports from toxicology," his administrative assistant reported. "Looks like victim number six was drugged with Risperine prior to taking a pistol to his head. I'm e-mailing you the report. Better be careful with what you eat and drink."

After ending the call, he checked his e-mail and opened the report his assistant had sent. This case was different from the rest, as if the murderer was purposely breaking a pattern. Instead of using drugs to kill, she used drugs to gaslight the victim into killing himself. The only reason this case was linked to the rest was due diligence by the victim's family.

Oscar Middleton was not the type to commit suicide. He had a comfortable life living on the beach in Hilton Head, had three loving sons and an active social life. Though in his seventies, he still golfed several times a week and played tennis. Everything was fine until he met Evelyn.

Evelyn claimed to be a widowed schoolteacher. According to his sons, he met her while spending a Season at The Chautauqua Institution. Within nine weeks they went from acquaintances to engaged. So enamored was he that he moved her into his upscale Hilton Head home. Only after marrying her in a quiet civil ceremony did he inform his sons. They were livid and suspicious from the start. Their father had never been irrational and compulsive.

The sons, with families of their own, observed their father during family visits and noticed his decline. Instead of the new, younger wife adding vitality, she seemed to be draining it. Oscar gave up golf, his social life, and became a recluse. When he was found in his car, shot in the head with a pistol, everyone suspected depression. Everyone, except his eldest son, who insisted on toxicology reports and an investigation. An overzealous coroner confirmed his suspicions. Evelyn had taken her share of the estate and mysteriously disappeared.

It was determined that Oscar had been drugged with Risperine over a period of time, altering his brain chemistry. Evelyn was discovered to be an alias, as the person with the name had been deceased for years and her identity stolen. Interesting was the fact that no one had a photograph of her. She had insisted on not having photographs taken because she was camera shy.

The woman in question was a force to be reckoned with. She knew pharmaceuticals and medicine, understood police procedures, how to cover her tracks and vanish, and especially how to lure unsuspecting men to their deaths like a "Siren." He had termed the investigation "Siren", after the tale of sea goddesses who lured sailors to their deaths with their beauty and love calls.

Six murders, over the course of six years were orchestrated by a cunning woman. All of the victims had a link to The Chautauqua Institution. His job was to prevent the seventh.

"Why the hell does this woman need to murder more men when she's sitting on an estimated $20 million in cash?" he asked aloud, yet he knew the answer.

This case had nothing to do with money. Money was just the reward, the trophy. She had to be exacting revenge for some past wrong, something that triggered her to kill and keep killing somehow to avenge it. Hers was mental illness and vengeance taken to the extreme.

CHAPTER 5

As Darrin walked the manicured grounds of the Institution, his mind was bombarded with memories. He had been born and raised on the grounds, and had witnessed its transformation from a sleepy village into an upscale summer resort. His roots were planted here for generations, beginning with the wood platform tent cottages that provided the original lodging. His ancestors had survived the failures and successes that laid the groundwork for the prestigious educational enclave it had become.

He couldn't think of the past without Katy. She was such an integral part of his history.

Strolling down blacktopped South Lake Road through the Children's School with its old clapboard buildings, he was reminded of their meeting. Her mother had inherited a summer home and enrolled her in the Children's School, an educational camp for children aged three to five. His parents could only afford two weeks.

When Katy walked into the classroom with her hands on her hips, sassy smile and pigtails, she acted as if she owned the place. He had found her to be the most interesting creature he had ever met. Granted, he was five at the time, as was she, but he was smitten.

They became inseparable playmates and friends. At age seven, they moved up to Boys' and Girls' Club, the oldest day camp in the country, founded in 1893. It was where he learned how to swim, sail, kayak, and canoe, and where he experienced first love, "puppy love."

As preteens, bodies and minds transformed, and friendship turned into romance. He would abandon chores to sneak off for bike rides with her. He introduced her to the sprawling, landscaped grounds, red brick walks, paved and unpaved paths, the hills to trudge up and cruise down and the famous Thunder Bridge. They spent hours in the woods seated on tree stump benches near the Ravine chatting. Subsequent summers came and went as he waited in eager anticipation of her nine-week visit. His parents found it cute, while her parents raised their eyebrows.

As he peered at the docks of Heinz Beach in front of the Boys' and Girls' Clubhouse and Heinz Fitness Center, he was reminded of their first kiss. One evening they sat on the wood dock, their feet dangling, rippling the water. Under the moonlight, he reached out, drew her to him and kissed her. She was the first girl he kissed, and he never forgot the gentle sweetness of her lips and the way their bodies melded together like pieces of a puzzle. The act was so natural and comfortable. He had experienced his first erection and she was as startled as he. They drew apart, not mentioning the newly discovered sensations of puberty.

Memories of their first sexual encounter flashed in his mind. As teens, they snuck up into the attic of The Carter Inn and experienced their first taste of lovemaking, if that awkward learning experience could be equated with the term. The bare mattress had been as dusty as the space. The softness of her body crushed against his and the euphoric release after being inside and a part of her was something he would never forget. The thought alone brought back feelings that had long been dormant.

He strolled by the venerable Athenaeum Hotel, and remembered how they held hands and discussed the beauty of the place. The grand dame on the lakefront still held her beauty. The multiple stories, straight mansard roof, tall windows, slender posts, carved banisters, expansive veranda facing the lake, gardens, and sweeping lawn exuded Victorian elegance.

Katy had mentioned how it was the perfect setting for a wedding. She had envisioned bridesmaids in flowing chiffon gowns posed on the curving double baroque staircase surrounding the fountain that led up to the lakeside veranda. They, in their finery would be standing on the landing, the minister at the rail. Her gown would be white satin while he wore black tie and tails. Instead of being frightened of the prospect, he had considered it a given. Katy was his everything. She was his past, present, and future.

He shoved his hands in the pockets of his cargo pants as he walked up North Lake Road. Cyclists sped by. He passed the bocce and shuffleboard courts and the Sportsmans' Club, with its rental kayaks and purple martin birdhouses. He peered out at grassy Miller Park and the Miller Bell Tower. The 75-foot-high bell tower, constructed in 1911 was the Institution's landmark. Of North Italian style, the Harvard brick structure housed a clock and 14-bell chimes that were played at various times throughout the day. Nostalgia overwhelmed him.

He saw that the iron and wood park bench under the famous Sycamore tree was still at the Children's Beach. He smiled at the memory of where they had dalliances with moonlight shimmering on the water. The deep kisses, the feel of her small breasts under her shirt and how she had placed her hands on the bulge in his slacks.

Where had the time gone?

What happened to *them?*

Life didn't turn out as dreamed. Did it ever? For anyone?

He shrugged.

The chimes began to play in the bell tower as they had at 8 a.m., noon, and 6 p.m. during the Season. Carolyne

Benton, the Chimemaster, selected favorite songs, either from concert, choir or opera performances or requests, to play on her tiny keyboard at the tower's base. The melodies, children's songs, hymns to popular music rafted through the Institution. He stood to listen as "Memory" rang out. How fitting, he surmised as melancholy overcame him.

He trudged up the hilly Vincent, passing meticulously restored Victorian homes with porches of wicker furniture, rocking chairs, and hanging planters overflowing with geraniums and ivy. As he made his way toward Bestor Plaza, he perused perennial gardens with black-eyed susans and hydrangeas in white, pink, blue, and purple hues.

The Plaza was the center of activity at the Institution, like a grassy quadrangle on a college campus surrounded by notable structures: The Colonnade office building and shops, the St. Elmo apartments, Smith Memorial Library, Post Office, and the popular Chautauqua Book Store. In the center was the Bestor Fountain, the center of which were carved figures representing the Institution's ideals of knowledge, music, art, and religion, with carved fish spraying water from each corner. Concrete planters of sunny pansies added color, neat hedges a hint of privacy.

He selected an iron and wood bench and parked himself. Back to work. Children were tossing a Frisbee. Raucous dogs were barking at one another as anxious owners pulled at leashes. Young musicians scurried by carrying hard instrument cases. A bevy of dancers pirouetted by the fountain as children played in the spray. A newspaper boy hawked papers, "*Chautauquan Daily*, seventy-five cents. Catch up on the day's events!" Couples held hands. Harried mothers pushed strollers that rumbled on the brick walks. Teens had cell phones plugged in their ears. Men and women of all ages dashed by as if on a mission.

He observed all of this life and felt as dead as the victims. Never had he thought so strongly that life was passing him by. What did he have? A career. He lived and breathed F.B.I. How fitting that he would be assigned a serial murder case at the Institution, where he had experienced so many beginnings and endings, a place where he was never a guest but always an employee, once an innkeeper's son and now a Special Agent. Others came for recreation yet he was never afforded that luxury. He was here to profile people and track a killer.

As he watched the flurry of activity and people around him, he began to think it absurd that a serial killer lurked in his midst. Everyone appeared so wholesome and decent.

Darrin had to admit that ever since he reached puberty, he hadn't had any difficulty in finding women to date. He knew that he had natural charm and an easygoing manner that women liked. Working out in the gym, dressing well, and maintaining intellectual conversation didn't hurt either. As Brantley Wentworth, he also came across as successful and insanely wealthy.

Initiating conversation with women was too easy at the Institution. Sitting in the amphitheater prior to lectures and performances allowed time for small talk with those seated nearby. Attending the programs at the Hall of Philosophy afforded more mingling. Just walking down the streets or sitting at park benches afforded company and conversation. Waiting in line for ice cream or sharing tables at the Brick Walk Café, or coffee at the Gazebo was a way to meet people. Some of the people were single women. One of them could be his suspect.

Seated on a park bench at Bestor Plaza, he observed other men and how they picked up women. The most effective ploy was having a cute dog on a leash. Women were suckers for dogs, and stopped to pet them and chat. A man with a dog, after all, had to be rather respectable and kind.

"I don't have a dog," he muttered.

"Excuse me," a soft woman's voice interrupted him from his thoughts.

He met the gaze of a very plain bespectacled woman, her face devoid of any cosmetics, and rather sallow and as plain as her pale brown eyes. A salt and pepper chin-length bob framed her face.

As she sat next to him on the green park bench, he noticed her petite frame and prim and proper manner as she crossed her hands on her lap.

"Were you asking about dogs?" she inquired.

"I was just talking to myself. I guess as long as I don't answer myself I'm all right," he answered with a chuckle, observing her.

"There are a lot of dogs here," she said. "I'm more of a crazy cat lady myself."

He wondered why this forty-something woman would start talking and sit next to him. Either she was desperate or had a motive. He couldn't rule anyone out. This was going to be fun. Right. He was allergic to cats.

"Really? How many do you have?"

She broke into a gap-toothed smile. "About six."

"I wouldn't call that a crazy number."

"Had to leave my babies at home. A neighbor is looking in on them."

"Where's home?"

"Right now, Ohio. And you?"

"California."

"That's a long trip. You must really like it here."

"I don't know. It's my first Season."

Her eyes lit up. "You're here for the Season, too?"

"Yes, nothing like a nice leisurely vacation. If I like it, I may just end up purchasing some property."

Her eyes sparkled more. "I see. I'm staying at the Athenaeum. Actually, I was just walking there when I heard you speak."

“I was going to head down to the lake. Perhaps I can escort you?”

“I’d like that. I’d like that a lot.”

He did not like it. Actually, it was the last thing he wanted to do. She was taking his bait either as a lonely woman or as a suspect. He couldn’t rule anyone out and had to follow all leads. She was as good as any.

He kept reminding himself that she was a possible suspect as they walked side by side down the steep incline leading toward the Athenaeum and the lake. She, in her denim jumper and Birkenstocks with socks, and he in his cargo shorts, tee shirt and tennis shoes. He listened intently as she talked about her loneliness after losing her husband, and lack of children and family. Her whining voice was annoying but her story raised his suspicions. He acted interested to keep her talking.

Out of the corner of his eye, he saw Katy placing a rug over the carved banister of the wraparound front porch of her inn. He would have rather spent the time chatting with her and catching up. With her hand, she batted the rug, releasing dust motes. A gray tee hugged her chest and the way it was tucked in her jeans accented her small waist. He was tempted to wave the woman off and join her instead. However, he would never catch his suspect if he spent all of his time with Katy. She shook her head as he passed. He wondered what she thought about him and this animated woman walking together as if entranced with one another. He was grateful when they approached the maroon canopied entrance to the hotel and they parted, but not before setting up a time to meet for the Symphony concert in the evening.

That evening, he gathered seat cushions from the inn’s lobby for the Symphony. The benches in the amphitheater were rather hard on the back for any length of time. He couldn’t subject Mildred, the woman he met at Bestor, to the pain. He dreaded the evening that would be better spent on the computer than escorting some plain woman to a violin concerto and Schumann concert.

"Someone has a hot date," Katy said, grasping a mug of coffee as she appeared at the front counter.

"I wouldn't call it hot by any means," he replied with a smirk.

"You are certainly making moves around here." She set down her mug.

"What are you talking about?" He stared at her.

"Well, let's see. A woman was here to see you earlier. She said that she met you at the Brick Walk and wanted to continue an interesting conversation on Descartes. Another woman dropped off a book on the Supreme Court for your "borrowing pleasure," her words and not mine. Tonight, you are taking two cushions to the Symphony." She laughed.

"I don't see where my personal life should concern you."

"Actually, I'm finding it rather entertaining. Some of these women are old enough to be your mother."

"I have an explanation, but this isn't the time."

He gathered the cushions and rushed out the door into the misty evening air. Why Katy? Why now?

CHAPTER 6

Katherine sat at the front counter and looked down at the bills that needed to be paid. No sooner had she had income, her expenses would obliterate any profit. The fun of ownership.

"Honey, where can a woman get a drink around here?" a honey-blonde with a Southern drawl asked.

Katherine peered up from her papers and her thoughts to meet the woman's sparkling blue gaze. Her eyes were about the only thing natural about her. Her face, jaw line, and neck were overly taut and even her Pamela Anderson figure couldn't hide her obvious age. Her veined hands, even with perfectly manicured nails, betrayed her.

"Well, a few of the restaurants sell glasses of wine but only if you order a meal. Otherwise, you have to drive off the grounds to Mayville's liquor store," she answered.

"Are you kidding me?"

"Hey, unless you befriend someone who's willing to share. Regulars all have caches of beer, wine, and booze."

"I swear, this place is reminding me of Prohibition."

The woman wasn't *that* old. Katherine smiled.

"The Institution likes to preserve an old fashioned family atmosphere."

"Looks like I landed in a dry state." The woman sighed and left.

The joys of being an innkeeper, answering the same mundane questions over and over from clueless tourists.

Last Season's doozey came from an elite Wall Street banker and his family. After reserving a suite months in advance, he came storming into the lobby confronting her.

"The accommodations are not up to our standards. The fixtures are old and the furniture musty antiques. Nothing is new or modern. Aren't there any five-star accommodations here?" he screamed.

She told him about the uniqueness of the Institution but he still requested a full refund and she obliged. He still had the nerve to dis her and the Institution on a prominent travel web site, venting that the place was out of touch. He didn't get it. Some people never did. If you want Las Vegas, go to Las Vegas. The Institution was for educational, spiritual, and recreational pursuit, not for carousing.

Darrin ambled into the lobby from outside. He looked almost as disappointed as the irate banker. His hands were shoved into the pockets of his cargo shorts and he shrugged. He appeared headed for upstairs until noting her and approached the counter.

"The work never stops, huh?" he asked.

She met his gaze, noting the crow's feet at the corners of his weary eyes.

"You know what they say, no rest for the wicked," she said.

"I've always wondered about the identity of the elusive, they," he replied.

"I should think that you more than anyone would know the answer."

He cocked his head. "Why?"

"Come on, I've been watching you. I've ruled out your being hard-up, a pervert, or a gigolo."

Katherine had been observing Darrin as he came and went and made his rounds at the Institution. He appeared to be a man on a mission. The mission, however, seemed strange.

He laughed. "A what?"

"My guess is that you're an undercover cop on a top secret mission that somehow involves women."

With his dashing good looks, finding a younger date would be easy. He didn't appear to be a male hooker. Maybe it was her habit of watching criminal dramas that he exhibited the attributes of law enforcement. When not stalking the grounds, he was making inquiries and spending a lot of time on his computer, hidden away in his room or on his private porch. His secrecy and insistency as being addressed by his alias added to her conclusion. She was finding him rather entertaining.

His wide-eyed reaction gave him away before he could answer.

"Very observant."

"So, I'm right?" She winked. "Don't worry, I won't blow your cover. Maybe I can help. After all, innkeepers are pretty good judges of people and character."

He leaned on the counter. "Katy, you have always been too smart for your own good."

"Two heads are better than one."

"I don't work with partners," he scoffed.

"Informers?"

"I really don't want you involved in this. It's my assignment and I either sink or swim … alone."

"Hey, I saved you from drowning once." She reminded him. "Remember when your kayak capsized and you were trapped underneath at camp? Who swam under water to rescue you? Who pounded the water out of you so you could breathe?"

He smiled. It was more mouth-to-mouth. "Okay, once. This is a secret operation, and I'm under strict orders for the safety and reputation of the Institution."

"Sounds all legalese to me. Guess what? You've been away from here for a long time and some things have changed. I live here, know a lot of people, a lot of gossip, and hell of a lot more about the place than you. My guess is that you have nine weeks to catch up. I already have over twenty years of experience to share. My other guess is that if you don't have this crime solved in nine weeks, you and your career will be history. Perhaps, with my assistance, things can proceed faster?"

What the hell did she just say and commit herself to? The words just came out. She really did watch too many crime shows. She was an innkeeper and not an investigator. She already had enough on her plate with the operation of the inn and its expenses.

"Hmmm ..." He raised his finger to his lips. She could almost see the gears turning in his head. "You've made some valid points, though they are not part of F.B. I. protocol."

Oh damn, she thought, he's F.B.I. This was not a run-of-the-mill crime like theft or assault. The Institution had never experienced more than petty crime, until now, apparently.

Looking around to be assured that no one was watching, he reached into a pocket of his cargo pants and withdrew a leather bi-fold. He opened it and placed it before her on the counter.

The badge glinted in the light from the nearby banker's lamp. She read the credentials: Darrin Franklin Carter, Special Agent, F.B.I.

She met his serious gaze.

"I'm investigating a series of murders," he stated bluntly, his tone and manner so serious that shivers crept up from her spine to head.

"Murders? Here?" Considering their shared past, the thought made her dizzy.

"Murders can and do occur in the most utopian of places."

"I don't know of any here. Do I have a reason to be concerned?"

"No. However, it's paramount that you keep the situation and my real identity a secret."

"My lips are sealed. I'm not exactly the most social person."

He put the bi-fold away. "Katy, the case does involve women. I'm not looking for a date. I'm stalking a serial killer before she strikes again."

"She?"

He nodded. "If you notice any prospects, let me know. Here, I'll give you my private cell number. If you have any suspicions or concerns, call me."

She pulled out her cell and they exchanged numbers.

"It must be like looking for a needle in a haystack." He had his work cut out for him. Only nine weeks.

"It is."

"If you want my help, I'm here for you."

"Thanks, I may be needing all the help I can get." He walked away and up the stairs.

CHAPTER 7

Watching Darrin come and go provided a form of entertainment seldom seen on the grounds. His popularity with the ladies was growing by the day. He had dates for the morning worship service, morning lectures, lunch, the 2 p.m. lecture in the Hall of Philosophy, perusing the newest installations at Strohl and Kellogg-Fowler art galleries, dinner, and the evening's entertainment. In between, he had strolls to the lake and chats on Bestor Plaza. Most of the women were older than he. Not that it mattered. A good looking man who appeared to have money flashed on the radar of desperate widows, divorcees, and spinsters. Darrin, though, looked weary and his investigation appeared to be a lesson in futility. There were so many women desperate for male companionship, how could he possibly find the one bad apple in such a vast orchard?

Speaking of the devil. As she sat composing a grocery list on her perch behind the front counter, sipping a cup of afternoon green tea, Darrin appeared in the doorway. As he entered, he let the screen door shut with a bang. The act seemed to match his mood. His lips were pursed tight, brows up and eyes ablaze.

He caught her gaze. "I need a break and I need it now. You're joining me for lunch … off the grounds."

"Excuse me?" She set down her porcelain mug.

"We are going to lunch. I hear that Webb's is a nice place." He stood in front of her, hands shoved in his shorts' pockets.

“I really shouldn’t leave my post.”

“Bullshit.”

“What?” Why was he after her?

“I’ve observed you. Enough hiding behind that desk. You could use a break and a change of scenery and you know it.”

“I have work to do.” She pointed to the list. She could use a change of scenery, yet rarely left her post due to finances and the fear that something would happen to the inn, her only asset, in her absence.

“The other inns leave their desks unattended during the day. Guests are at programs and not in their rooms. Put up an out sign and let’s go.”

“I’m not an other inn. I do business my way.”

“Katy, the inn will be here when you get back.”

He was staring, and she knew that he could read her thoughts. She was paranoid because of the past, their past. Her biggest fear was that history would repeat itself and that she would once again be a victim. It wasn’t rational, she knew. It wore on her mind and prevented her from freeing herself from the inn and from her memories.

“Come on, Katy. I need to get out of here and I’d like some company.”

“I’d say that you’ve been having more than enough company and should be seeking solitude.” She thought of the other women.

“The right company. A diversion. It’s time we play catch-up.”

“My story isn’t that interesting.” She wasn’t sure if she was ready to discuss her troubled past.

“Katy, we had some amazing memories. Don’t let one bad one ruin your present and your future.”

She bit her bottom lip. He was angling too close to home and she shifted in her seat.

“What do you say? Live dangerously.” He smiled that arresting smile that had charmed her as a child and as a teen. It had always been so difficult, actually impossible, to turn him down.

She stood with a sigh. "Darrin, you win. You always win."

He chuckled. "Not always."

That was true. He didn't win her.

Webb's Captain's Table was a popular tourist restaurant in Mayville across from Chautauqua Lake. It was part of Webb's Resort, a mixture of hotel, candy factory, Cottage Collection Gift Shop and Café, and miniature golf course. The restaurant had the dark, wood-grained ambiance found in finer restaurants with a nautical theme.

Darrin selected a private booth for quiet conversation. Ever since he saw Katy at the inn, he had wanted to get her alone to talk. For so many years he had wondered what had become of her. His curiosity had been piqued when he discovered that she had returned to the Institution. She was the last person he expected to see. Hers had to have been an interesting journey.

He looked across at her face. Though tired, she wasn't shopworn. She had the glow of youth, but the wisdom of age. The defeat in her eyes revealed an inner sadness and the hesitancy in her voice, fear.

"You won," she said. "I'm here." She clasped her hands primly on the tabletop.

"I always win." He smiled. His winning had been a childhood and youth joke in their shared past.

"I rarely leave the grounds during the Season, only to pick up groceries and run errands. Operating the inn is my life."

"Okay, I'm cutting to the chase now that I have you to myself. What the hell ever possessed you to return to the

Institution?" The question had been on his mind ever since his arrival.

"I hadn't a choice. It's the only thing I inherited and the only thing I have of any value. As you recall, my father lost his life, reputation, and fortune due to the fire. I also lost my mother. The house was all I had. When I turned twenty-one, it was mine."

"You could have sold it for a tidy profit."

"And then what? I had nothing. I had nowhere to go. It's the only place that held my family history, my mother's legacy, and the only fond memories I ever had. Selling it would be giving away part of my soul."

The way her voice cracked and trembled made him realize how difficult things had been. He listened as she explained how she had taken out loans to renovate the place and how she had struggled to maintain it. Life wasn't fair. At least it wasn't fair to Katy Morrow.

"I had lived on the charity of relatives for too long," Katy explained. "Getting the deed meant freedom."

"If I recall, after the fire and your mother's suicide, you were taken in by your aunt and uncle in Connecticut." He remembered her tears of anguish over the loss of the only life she had ever known. At that time, he suffered the loss of his parents and the only girl he had ever loved, if it was love. At the time, it sure the hell felt like it. It was an emotional time in both of their lives.

"I never fit in. I was treated like a burden. They were okay but I wasn't their child. Instead of going away to college like my cousins, I had to work. My aunt treated me like a servant. I left their home at eighteen and was on my own. Ironically, I learned about the hospitality business by working in it. I began as a chambermaid and worked my way up to desk clerk and eventually assistant general manager. Then, of all things, an attorney contacted me about the deed to the house at the Institution. I thought that the property had been sold long ago. No one ever told me about it being held in a trust. With my experience, what other alternative did I have but to turn it into an inn?"

"That's a remarkable story. It seems that someone up there was guiding you."

Her eyes were glistening and he swallowed hard. He reached over and grasped her arm. She didn't draw away but let him hold her arm as she began to weep. He moved his hand to withdraw a handkerchief from his pants' pocket and handed it to her. She dabbed her eyes.

"Thanks." She held the kerchief in her hand. "Sorry, I didn't mean to cry."

"There's no reason to be sorry. The tears are warranted."

A waiter appeared.

"We still need a few minutes," Darrin said.

The waiter nodded and left.

"I guess we'd better check out the menu," Darrin said.

"I've never been here, if you can believe it." Katy's lips still trembled.

After ordering, Katy was more composed, though she still grasped the linen kerchief.

"I never stopped thinking about you," Darrin said. "I always wondered if we'd ever meet again."

"I often wondered about you, too."

"We never really had time to say goodbye." After the fire, life had been so disjointed, frenetic, and chaotic. She had been whisked away by her relatives and he by his. After that fated night, they had never seen each other until he walked into her inn.

"So, Darrin, how did you become and F.B.I. agent? Did the fire influence your decision?" she asked.

He pondered a moment and stroked his chin. "Actually, the fire motivated me to enter law enforcement. My aunt and uncle never had children and when they took me in, they adopted me as their own. I graduated with a degree in psychology. Wonder why? Worked as a cop while attending graduate and law school. Got accepted into the

F.B.I. and I'm based in New York City. It's ironic that I would be assigned a case at the Institution."

"We've both come full circle, haven't we?"

"Sure seems that way." Fate had a strange sense of humor.

"Fate had us survive the fire."

Her words brought silence. Some things were better thought than said.

He hadn't enjoyed a lunch out in a long time. Being a workaholic, he only went to lunch with fellow agents, members of law enforcement or informants. His social life had been relegated to quick, non-committal hook-ups. Being with Katy was like reliving old times, when they were both young and carefree. It made him realize how little people really appreciate their childhood and youth. That time in life is so short. Age brought experiences both good and bad, loss and sadness, disappointment and grief, responsibility and regret.

Returning to the inn, Katy went back to her front counter. She took down the 911-cell phone contact sign. "Maybe I'll use it again. Getting away actually felt good."

"Everyone needs a change of pace." He smiled.

"Thank you for lunch and the company. It's the first time I've ever discussed my past and my life."

"We've been on the same journey. Life after tragedy."

She sighed. "Life goes on, doesn't it?"

"Life does go on and you can't let is pass you by. You can't keep living here like a hermit, Katy." He didn't want to lecture her but she had so much to offer and was hiding.

She didn't respond but shuffled papers. He took it as a cue to leave and turned to go upstairs to his suite to work on his laptop.

CHAPTER 8

Katherine pondered his words as she lay in her Jenny Lind bed that night begging for sleep, but awake with memories. He had opened the floodgates with their afternoon conversation. Emotions she had repressed for so many years reappeared with a vengeance. Tossing and turning, tears streamed from her eyes as she blotted them with tissue after tissue.

Life sucked!

She lost her parents and was sent away with relatives who treated her like a charity case and not family. Though they had money, they lavished it on their biological children, providing her with mere necessities. She worked summers when school was out for small luxuries like a movie ticket or trinket. When she turned eighteen, she was shown the door while her cousins attended college. They got an education while she got the shaft. It was no wonder that her favorite fairy tale as a child was *Cinderella.*

Her inheritance was spent on legal fees and judgements. Darrin was granted a huge sum by the courts in a civil case brought by his parents' estate, and rightfully so. Her father, after all, caused the fire that killed his parents. It didn't matter that her parents also died that night.

Her future died in that fire. The Morrows were old money dating back to the Mayflower. Her mother, Julia, was a debutante with an enviable inheritance, and her father an Ivy League Wall Street investment banker. She had been born into wealth and privilege. There was the Long Island mansion, and the Chautauqua summer home that had been in her mother's family since the Institution's founding. She had been educated in private schools, tutored in French, and played the piano. There were thoughts of an education at Harvard or Yale. Her future had been filled with promise.

It all ended that cool July evening when she had just turned fifteen. Being an only child, her birthdays were special. Mother had gone out of her way to personally prepare her favorite foods and bake and decorate a chocolate cake. Her birthday celebration had ended with the Symphony's traditional rendition of the 1812 Overture, complete with the synchronized popping of paper bags and after, watching fireworks explode over the lake on the Fourth of July. Chautauqua Lake had been traditionally circled by red flares, the "ring of fire," and the chimes played patriotic songs as fireworks exploded over the lake from Mayville and surrounding communities. Little did she know that later, in the wee hours of the next morning, other fireworks would erupt.

The Queen Ann Victorian was eerily quiet when Katy had gone to bed after her day of celebrating. She was awakened to the voices of her parents arguing. It wasn't the first time she heard them raise their voices in anger. Her parents had a tumultuous oil and vinegar relationship. When with her, they were loving and amicable. When alone, they were volatile. She lived her life on pins and needles and suffered her sadness alone and in silence.

That evening, she heard their bedroom suite door open. Her mother was begging her father to stay but he screamed that he had other plans. The words "Carter Inn" screeched from her mother. Her father had a habit of leaving them alone and disappearing into the night, only to reappear after breakfast. His footsteps could be heard stomping down the stairs, ending with the front door slamming. Her mother's howling cries echoed through the house. Katy often sobbed softly before falling into slumber. This night was different. The agony of her mother's cries was more pronounced. She lay in bed crying but awake.

The abrupt silence from her parents' bedroom caused her sit up with concern. Only the crickets chirping outside her window could be heard. Her heart palpitated and a cold sweat enveloped her. A sense of foreboding penetrated her body.

Trembling with fear, she wanted to crawl into her mother's warm embrace. Perhaps she and her mother could comfort each other in the still of darkness.

Stepping out of bed and into the hall, she approached her parents' suite and hesitated before opening the door. Moonlight lit the salon and the bedchamber beyond with a hazy azure glow. She tiptoed inside in silence, crossing the Victorian era salon and into the bedchamber. Approaching the bed, she saw that the sheets and quilt were in disarray but the bed was empty. Her mother wasn't tucked in.

The nightlight in the bathroom was on and the door slightly ajar.

"Mommy?" she asked, acting more of a child than a teen of fifteen.

No answer.

Her heartbeat intensified and her palms grew sweaty. She swallowed hard before pushing open the door.

Her mother's bare leg was dangling out of the bathtub, pale as alabaster and still. Shivers ran up her spine and down her arms.

"Mommy?" she repeated, approaching the tub with caution.

The fabric shower curtain was drawn. With fear and trepidation, she took a deep breath and drew it open.

The blood-curdling scream was her own. Her mother lay motionless in the empty, dry tub. Her face was pale, her lips a tinge of blue. Her ivory silk nightgown was soaked in blood. A bloody pocketknife, her father's, rested on her stomach. Her wrists were slashed, coated in blood, as were her still hands.

"Mommy. Why, Mommy?" She choked on her words.

She reached out to stroke her mother's face and hair, knowing that her mother was dead, for her blue eyes were open in a dull vacant stare. Her mouth gaped open as if in frozen pain. She drew her hand away as her body trembled.

Rising, she grew nauseous. She knelt at the commode and dry heaved as tears rolled down her cheeks. She stood, hugging herself.

"Daddy?" she screamed. Her mother had begged him not to go to The Carter Inn. The Carter Inn!

"Daddy what have you done? Daddy!"

She rushed out of the room.

She went to the telephone and dialed 911. Without waiting for authorities, she ran out of the house barefoot and in her cotton nightgown in the chilled, misty air of the quiet Institution grounds. She had to see her daddy and tell him what happened. He had to know what he had caused.

The Carter Inn, the sign read. The Inn was owned and operated by Darrin's parents, as it had been for generations before them. The quaint Victorian Inn with its gingerbread trim, balconies and distant views of the lake was one of the most desirable on the grounds. The Inn always brought happy memories until the night of her mother's suicide.

She stepped in the front door on her tiptoes. The lobby was quiet and empty. The amber glow of a dim table lamp on the front desk afforded the only light. She slunk up the stairs where the guest rooms were located. When she heard her father's booming voice, he was arguing with a woman. First, there was a fight with her mother. Now, a disagreement with another woman? Her father had the audacity to be with another woman. That was why her mother had been upset? The room had been located at the far end of a corridor, private and away from the others. She pressed her ear to the door. She could still remember the conversation.

"I'm leaving you," her father said in a calm steadfast tone. "I can't put up with this nonsense."

"You can't leave me now. You know I'm pregnant," the woman said with angst.

"How do I know whose bastard it is?"

"You're the bastard!" There was the sound of an object, possibly a vase, hitting the wall. There was a scuffle and the woman screamed.

"I'll choke you until you lose it," he threatened. There was a crash and another scream.

"Shit!" Her father was scurrying around, as the scent of something burning and smoke crept from under the door.

"Damn candles!" He screamed again.

Katherine grew concerned. Candles were banned on the Institution grounds. A fire amongst all of the old clapboard buildings would be a catastrophe. Aged dry wood in buildings without sprinklers, like the Carter Inn was a feared disaster.

A smoke alarm went off. In a panic, Katherine pushed at the door and it opened. She met her father's stunned gaze, dark and wide with fear. He lunged forward before flames engulfed him and ignited the room. Though she couldn't see the woman, her screams were deafening. A ball of orange and yellow fire erupted from the room and rolled into the hall. She ran from it, screaming. Other guests scrambled from rooms with panicked screams

All she remembered was Darrin grabbing her, carrying her in his arms and rushing her out of the building and into the crisp night air. She remembered how he held her close as they watched the inn erupt in a blaze of orange and red flames. The acrid smoke choked her lungs and made her eyes water. Her nightgown was singed, and a blistering pain throbbed on her chest, stomach and thighs. Knowing she was injured, she hid the fact. The gravity of the situation was beyond the physical. Darrin was more important than her pain and she clung to him. His eyes were transfixed on the inn. Tears rolled down his cheeks. He whimpered, calling for his parents while holding her tight.

The siren of the volunteer fire department was blaring and soon, the sirens and flashing lights of fire trucks and rescue squads appeared on the scene. Fire trucks from the Institution, Mayville, and surrounding communities worked together to contain the flames. People were milling around in nightclothes as residents and guests from surrounding inns and homes came out to observe the unfolding nightmare with their screams, wails, and chattering conversation

Flames shot into the night sky as outfitted firemen grasping hoses doused them with water. The wood crackled and sputtered as the roof and then walls of the inn collapsed, resembling a bonfire more than a structure.

Just recalling the events of that evening caused her to tremble and break out into a cold sweat. Her heart pounded in her chest, as her eyes filled with tears. Katherine hugged herself and cried. This was a nightmare that occurred regularly throughout her life. Visions of her mother soaked in blood, of her father's startled expression, fire consuming him before he could utter a word, flames igniting the dark sky, of curdling screams and the roar of water from hoses trying to contain the fire. The fear, loss and the acrid scent of death permeated her senses and her brain. She hated night for fear of having it trigger the memory. She had to sleep with a nightlight on to keep the ghosts of the past at bay.

She wondered if Darrin suffered nightmares. He was there and had suffered loss as well. He lost his parents and his future.

The scope of the event came to light with dawn. In the morning, while everyone huddled in the lobby of the

Athenaeum hotel, a damage assessment and personal toll were revealed. Their parents were unaccounted for. She and Darrin sat on a sofa, clinging to one another in the drafty hotel lobby, knowing that they had lost the lives they had known and their innocence.

Against their objections, they were taken to the hospital in Westfield in separate rescue squads. Both had suffered burns in the fire that required hospitalization and treatment. The physical burns were treated, but the mental anguish would remain forever.

The fire had taken the lives of Darrin's parents. They had been trapped in the inn they so cherished and lovingly cared for. It burned down quickly with them inside, and only charred remains had been found. The same was said for Katherine's father and his paramour. The woman was a Seasonal guest at the Institution. Apparently, she had lit candles for ambiance. The ensuing altercation resulted in them catching fire to the drapes and the bed. The fire ignited the inn like a tinderbox, consuming guests trapped in upstairs rooms.

Katherine was taken in by her father's younger sister and only sibling. She was never to see the inside of the Chautauqua cottage until her inheritance. Darrin had been adopted by a loving aunt and uncle.

She swallowed hard, choking on tears and phlegm. How ironic that she would be the innkeeper, and he would be the guest.

CHAPTER 9

Darrin had a fitful sleep thinking about Katy and all that had transpired in their lives, together and alone. He wondered how their futures would have been had the fire not consumed their parents and their dreams. He was forced to reflect upon his past as vivid memories resurfaced.

He had been groomed to inherit the inn and to operate it, and he couldn't think of a more satisfying occupation. He loved the old building and its history, the antiques within it and the joy of meeting guests from around the country and from around the world. There were many regulars who were like family. Being an only child, he had never felt alone when the guests included other children.

The only time he was humbled was when he was with Katy. Hers was a different life. She was pedigreed and pampered. His life consisted of work, while hers was all play. Her parents owned a stately summer home. She was guest while he was the innkeeper.

Yet, they played together as children, attended school and camp together. As teens, they even snuck off for evening trysts. She was his first girlfriend and summer love. They used to share dreams about the future and how, together, they would create their happily ever after.

Reality, though, reared its ugly head. Her world did not include him. Privileged young women did not associate with the help. He was viewed as a servant by her parents, and nothing more. She was forbidden to associate with him once they reached puberty. Seeing each other had become increasingly difficult through the years. He knew that she would one day be sent off to some fancy college, where she would meet her blue-blooded destiny while he tended to the inn. He knew that one day, she would inherit the family home and he the family inn. The chasm between their two worlds would run deep and distant.

The fire changed everything. It was never more evident than in the here and now. In speaking with her, he sensed her sadness and the disappointment the change in her life's path had taken. He also sensed her loneliness.

Loneliness was something that he understood and could relate to. No matter how many people he met, and no matter the number of people he was surrounded by, he always felt alone. He never was a part of any circle. Yet, he liked it. He thrived when alone.

His aunt and uncle would chastise him and encourage him to join clubs and social circles in schools. He would join but keep an emotional distance. He never confided in anyone.

It was rather funny that the only person he had ever felt comfortable around and poured out his heart and soul to was Katy. No other person and no other woman came close.

For someone groomed to run an inn, surrounded by people, the fire had turned him into a loner. That personality served him well in law enforcement and in life. Investigating horrendous crimes demanded a hands-off, unemotional, and analytical approach. His profession had become his life and his life his profession.

He thought about Katy. It appeared that she, too, had become a bit of a recluse. She seemed fearful of leaving the inn, her comfort zone. Had the past really messed them both up, preventing them from experiencing normal relationships? As if he knew what normal really was. After all, here he was dating a bunch of women. Instead of essentially interviewing them as a potential mate, he was investigating them as a possible serial killer.

After waving off his latest subject, Darrin found Katy with a corn husk broom in one hand sweeping off the inn's front porch. She peered up at him with a smirk.

"Did you buy that Southern belle the drink she so desperately craved?" she asked.

He glanced at the woman who was walking down the path and back at Katy.

"You know her?" he asked.

"Not really, I just met her once and she was asking about booze."

He shook his head. The aging Southern bombshell had more on her mind than alcohol. He wouldn't go into *that* with Katy. There were many things that he would do for work, but having kinky sex with desperate, older women was not one of them.

"Glenda is quite a character," he replied.

"This place is filled with characters. I swear it's like most small towns, but this one has a revolving population." She leaned on her broom. He found the pose, along with her denim Bermuda shorts and snug white tee shirt sexy as hell. Feelings began to stir that he had kept repressed for a long time.

"So, any leads for me, partner?" he asked more as a tease than a serious inquiry.

She shook her head. "I think that you've met every available female here."

"I do think I've met all of the full Season residents. I've been more interested in those who are staying for the Season but are not property owners."

"The seekers and not the already moneyed?"

"Exactly. The difficult and scary part is that everyone seems so ordinary."

"Psychopaths tend to fit in, don't they?"

"Who's the investigator here?"

A guest at the inn stepped on to the porch. "Good afternoon."

"Good afternoon to you, too, Mr. Anderson," Katy replied.

The elderly man with the slow gait ambled across the painted wood floor to the porch swing.

Darrin looked at her and knew that she understood that the conversation had to change when guests were milling about.

"So what are your plans?" Katy asked.

"Another Symphony and another date."

"I hope that this one's special." She winked.

"Oh, she is."

Her head tilted in a curious and cute manner.

"I was wondering if you would join me this evening, Ms. Morrow? That is, if you haven't any other plans."

"I usually balance my books in the evening, and run the laundry."

"Make an exception this once. I can't bear another evening with a matron."

She sighed. "You are most persuasive."

"It's the secret to my charm with the ladies."

"Okay."

Darrin smiled. His idea to ask her was purely spur of the moment but her accepting his invitation was like winning the lottery. This was ridiculous. He was supposed to be hunting down a serial killer and not reuniting with his childhood sweetheart. He wasn't a guest, he was working. Oh hell, he knew what was said about all work and no play.

CHAPTER 10

Katherine asked herself over and over if she was nuts. What was she doing getting dressed in a floral sundress and sandals to attend a Symphony concert with Darrin? She even curled her hair and put on makeup for the occasion. She was usually lucky to dab on some lipstick. When was the last time she had actually worn a dress, let alone sandals? When was the last time she had ever attended any concert in the amphitheater? Crazy as it seemed, she lived on the grounds but never experienced any of the Season. She had lived vicariously through her guests. She was required to pay for a Season pass but viewed it more as a tax than a perk.

Damn Darrin. He had come back into her life and changed the atmosphere.

She assured herself that this was merely a friendly reunion with an old friend, and not a date. Right.

When Darrin appeared in the lobby, he looked as if he had just stepped out of shower and out of GQ. The crisp khaki pants fit as if tailored for him and the designer logo shirt with sweater knotted about his shoulders looked very preppie. He even wore loafers without socks. He was the poster boy for Ralph Lauren.

"Ready?" he asked.

She grabbed her small purse and sweater from the counter. "Ready."

"And, we can't forget these or we'll be sorry." Darrin grabbed two seat cushions before leaving the inn.

As they stepped off the porch, she said, "You must have been a Boy Scout. Be prepared."

"Hey, how did you guess? Eagle Scout." He chuckled.

The stroll down the brick walkway to the amphitheater was as pleasant as the weather. Katherine knew, though, that evening often came with a chill. Sitting in an open-air amphitheater for a couple of hours could make one cold in a hurry. They were scanned inside by volunteers and found aisle seats in the middle section.

Darrin set down the cushions on the ivory-painted bench, and they sat. Though there was plenty of room, the cushions brought them closer and she tingled as his thigh brushed against hers. He draped an arm across the back of the wood bench, across her shoulders as well and she shivered. She inhaled his scent of soap and shampoo, as if it were fine perfume. Had she really been without a man for so long that she forgot how special it was?

The orchestra was tuning up on the brightly lit stage for the evening's performance. The audience was filtering in with endless chatter. A woman seated in front of them was knitting, another perusing her Kindle. The man behind was chatting on his cell.

"Hi, " a woman greeted as she strode down the inclined aisle.

Another woman tripped but caught herself while looking over at him and winking.

"My, you have a fan club," Katherine said, finding the number of women who were familiar with him amusing and a bit disconcerting.

"Trust me, none of them is going to win my heart."

"Or wallet?"

"Shh … Tonight is play and not work." He looked over the evening's printed program, "The concert looks good …"

"Mahler is a fine composer."

"I'll take your word for it."

They listened to the orchestra, members clad in white with the conductor in a tailored black tux. The musicians were from symphonies around the world and during the nine weeks they became the Chautauqua Symphony Orchestra, affectionately known as the CSO. After the concertmaster tuned with his violin, the conductor appeared and a hush came over the amphitheater, and the musicians began to play.

During intermission, when the house lights came on, more women waved their way, and she was finding them quite annoying.

"What is wrong with them?"

"I know. They won't let go even when I'm on a date with someone else," he said.

"This isn't a date."

"Really? It sure looks like a date to me."

"Don't get any ideas. You're just an old friend I've reconnected with." She had to assure herself.

"What are you afraid of?"

"I'm not afraid of anything."

"I think that you've been self-sufficient for so long that you're afraid of actually losing control."

"How would you know?" He was right but she wouldn't admit it. She didn't want anyone and didn't need anyone.

"Because I'm the same way. We're too alike, you and I. We always have been and probably always will."

"Then this can't be a date because we're bad for each other." Or, good for each other? What was she thinking?

The lights dimmed and intermission was over. The concertmaster tuned the orchestra and the Symphony resumed.

After the concert, they walked on the brick walk that shimmered under white globe street lamps, the moon, and star lit sky. Katherine put on her sweater, with Darrin's help, as the air had a slight breeze and chill. He had donned his sweater as well.

"I keep forgetting how cold it gets at night here, even in the middle of summer," he said.

"I know. It's something I've had a hard time adjusting to. The lakes and altitude cause strange weather. Be glad you aren't here during the winter. It's brutal and the snow piles up to the second story. We sometimes get 300 inches."

"Lest you forget, I grew up here and am quite familiar with the long winters and snow."

She had forgotten. The tables had turned, and she had a difficult time adjusting. He had spent his early life on the grounds, and she her later years. She had to keep reminding herself.

"One thing I do remember is that tradition says that we must get an ice cream cone after the concert," he said, steering her toward the Brick Walk Café.

"I remember when this place was called the Refectory and wasn't so fancy," he recalled.

"The only thing certain in life is change and even the Institution is not immune, though change is implemented in subtle ways." Everything changed, including she and Darrin.

"Do you still like mint chocolate chip?" he asked.

How did he remember? "Actually, I do."

"On a sugar cone?"

"Yes."

"Hey, it was always my favorite, too." He winked.

After getting their ice cream cones, she followed Darrin to a park bench under a tree on Bestor Plaza. Even with people milling about, there was a serene silence in the night. The air held a mist with a fresh scent that wafted up from the lake. She drew in some air before tackling her cone.

"I don't know what it is but ice cream really tastes better here. There's something so special about it. It's not just ice cream, it's a feeling," he said.

"I know. It sort of goes with the entire Chautauqua experience, like going back in time when life was simpler, kinder, and less hurried."

"Like our youth."

She sighed. "So long ago."

As she licked her cone, swirling her tongue around to prevent the ice cream from melting on her hand, she caught him staring at her. After wondering what he was thinking, she felt her face grow hot. Not *that.* Oh, no, she was just eating ice cream with a friend. A very old friend. From the past.

They finished heir cones in silence.

Raindrops tickled her face.

"Well, I guess we should be heading back to the inn. It's going to rain," she said.

"It always rains here."

"I have an early morning. I have breakfast rolls to make, and laundry to throw in the wash." She stood, thinking of her chores and how she had to end the evening somehow, though she really didn't want it to end because it was the closest she had come to a date in years.

As they walked down Clark Brick Walk, the rain turned to drizzle. Of course, she had left her umbrella behind. She rattled on about her chores as they made their way toward the inn. He listened in silence.

"Will you ever stop talking?" he asked, startling her from her thoughts.

Before she could respond, he put one hand behind the small of her back, the other behind her neck, drawing her intimately close. As she gasped, his lips met hers in a hard and demanding kiss.

The act was so unexpected that she froze in disbelief. As his lips pressed against hers, their warmth and electricity were so delightful that she answered back. When did he learn to kiss like this? Soft as cashmere, his lips smothered hers with kisses. Slow, fast, deep, hard. He drew her tongue into his mouth to swirl with hers, gently nibbling with his teeth. More kisses led to deeper kisses. Tongues merged and lunged while she tingled from head to toe. She wrapped her arms around him, pulling at him as their bodies touched so intimately she could feel his erection harden against her.

His deep and passionate kisses melted her reserve. She had forgotten how stimulating and addictive his kisses could be. Time had aged him, but the lust of youth remained.

The rain had intensified and she hadn't noticed, so lost was she in the moment. He seemed oblivious to it as well.

"Damn, I knew this was the only way to shut you up," he whispered before trailing kisses to her ear, neck and collarbone before releasing her.

"It was effective," she had to admit. What in the world got into her? For the moment she forgot time and place. She wasn't fifteen, and they were not an item.

He smiled. "Time may change many things, Katy, but that wasn't one of them."

"We're getting wet," she said, swiping at rain dripping down her face.

"In more ways than one." He laughed, putting his arm around her shoulder as they quickened their pace. She was glad that he couldn't see her blush. The heat rising from her face mimicked that of other parts of her anatomy.

At the inn, Darrin pondered whisking her up to his room for an evening of lovemaking or a chaste kiss goodnight. His body was telling him one thing, his brain another. Slow and easy. After all of the trauma in her life and apprehension at their reunion, he thought it best to follow the latter.

In the lobby, he lowered his face to hers for a brief kiss. "Goodnight, Katy."

"Goodnight," she whispered.

He turned and went upstairs to his suite. Thoughts of Katy, their past and present, formed a kaleidoscope of memories in his mind. He undressed and fought sleep under the patchwork quilt. If only he were a guest on vacation. The reunion would have been exciting instead of bittersweet.

He knew that he had to get his mind off of Katy and focus on the job at hand. Grieving families, law enforcement, and the Institution were counting on him to nail a killer before she struck again.

So far, he didn't have any solid leads or evidence. The women he encountered all seemed desperate for male companionship, more than money or revenge. He was beginning to view himself as desperate as well. How crazy was it that when cookies, cakes, pies and candy were delivered to the inn for him by the ladies, he refused to taste them. Instead, he broke off samples and Fed-Ex'd them in a rush to the crime lab in Buffalo for evaluation. He was doing it so often that the scientists were calling him "king." They said that they were like taste testers for royalty. All of the goodies tested out as safe and edible. He felt bad having tossed such lovingly baked goods from Seasonal residents.

Maybe he was paranoid. He only drank beverages that were sealed and, if not, used test strips to be assured that they were not drug or poison laden. He watched his back, viewing everyone he met with suspicion.

Katy had no idea what he was up against. He wanted her kept out of it and often regretted telling her of his being an agent and of his assignment. It wasn't a matter of not trusting her, because he did. He just didn't want her affected by anything that would happen. If only he had selected another inn for the Season. Moving at this point would arise suspicion and there were few, if any, available Seasonal accommodations to suit his needs. His life was far too complicated in a place known for its simplicity.

CHAPTER 11

Katherine laughed. Another care package had arrived, addressed to Brantley Wentworth III. He sure had admirers who loved to bake. She guessed that they lived by the adage, a way to man's heart is through his stomach. From what she could tell, Darrin wasn't putting on weight from all of these sweets, since he looked as buff as ever.

She noticed. Ever since their kiss in the rain, he was on her radar. The lanky boy had certainly grown into a hunk of a man. She finally admitted her attraction to him. It took one kiss to ignite a flame that had lain dormant for too many years. She realized that he was the only man she had ever cared about. For years, she had avoided men and relationships. Being a loner was easier and safer. You didn't get hurt when only holding yourself accountable for your life.

Darrin had come and disrupted things, knocking her off balance. Her simple life no longer seemed so easy and carefree. Seeing Darrin multiple times a day made her heart race, brought a smile to her face, and filled her with longing. His confident swagger, masculine good looks, deep voice, and radiant smile she anticipated. Knowing how he kissed made her a hot woman with dreams of passion and love. She wondered how she would exist when he left at the end of the Season. Would life ever be the same with such a void? How could she cope with another loss?

"Special delivery," a young teen announced, pulling her from her thoughts.

He was holding a tray of cookies from a local bakery. Not another one, she thought.

"It's for a Mr. Wentworth."

"Of course," she replied. "Just set them on the counter."

He did and paused. Katherine reached under the counter and removed a dollar bill and gave it to the delivery boy.

"Thanks." He beamed and jaunted out of the inn and on his way.

She perused the array of delicacies under the plastic dome. Chocolate chip, oatmeal, fudge brownies, s'mores. She had never seen s'mores in a party tray before and hadn't had any since Girls' and Boys' Camp. Her stomach grumbled.

"He won't notice if I took one, would he? What's he going to do with all of these anyway?" she whispered.

Un-taping the dome, she lifted it and removed a s'more and placed it on a piece of paper. After, she replaced the lid and tape. No harm done.

She bit into the chocolate, graham cracker, and marshmallow confection and sighed. The taste and texture were almost orgasmic. She finished it off and eyed the others under the dome.

"No, no. One was enough."

She grabbed the platter, walked from the counter and went upstairs. Darrin's door was open and she walked in, placing the cookie tray on his dresser.

"Out of sight, out of mind," she said, proud of her restraint and left.

Darrin ambled into the lobby after the evening concert, and found Katy slunk over her counter. She looked asleep. Didn't the woman ever leave her post? She took dedication to her business to the extreme. This was not the way for a lovely young woman to spend her life.

"You're still up? You should be in bed," he said. *Yeah, with me?* Where did *that* come from?

She raised her head. Her hair was all disheveled and her face sanguine and parched. Either she was hung over or ill.

"Are you okay?" He came toward her. She looked like hell. This was not the same woman he had seen earlier that day.

"No. I either have the flu or a bad case of food poisoning," she mumbled. "The bathroom and I have become intimate companions."

What the hell? He had a light-bulb moment, and the thought made him tremble.

"What did you eat recently?"

"Soup, salad, and a s'more."

"A s'more?"

"Sorry, I stole one from your latest care package. It was so good. If I knew I was going to get sick, I would have eaten more of them."

He remembered the tray of cookies sitting on his dresser. He hadn't had time to send them out for analysis. Since they were from the Sweet Spot Café in Mayville, he didn't see any problem or hurry. Until now.

"You and I are making a trip to the clinic in Westfield." He made the split-second decision. If this had anything at all to do with his case, he wanted her to have immediate medical care.

"I'm not really up to a car ride."

"Honey, you don't have a choice."

He did something desperate. He arranged for a golf cart to take them to the main gate, where a police cruiser was waiting to take them to Westfield. He hoped that it was late enough as to not attract undue attention.

The clinic was expecting them, put her on an I.V. and conducted a blood test and took a urine sample. As per his orders, they analyzed the results quickly.

"Potent rat poison," the doctor on call said in a serious tone.

"Rat poison?" Katy asked, "What?"

How could Darrin explain to her that he was the intended victim? Of all of the care packages he had received, the only suspicious one was the one she sampled. What were the odds? It came from a popular bakery, a place that he was visiting the next morning with the cookie tray after he sent samples off to the lab. Damn it, he wasn't Betty Crocker.

The doctor stared at them. "Agent Carter, as per your request, I e-mailed the results to your crime lab."

"Crime lab?" Katy asked, shaking her head.

"Will she be okay?" Darrin asked. Katy still appeared foggy and lethargic.

"She'll be fine. She needs to drink plenty of liquids to continue to flush out her kidneys. She's lucky she just ate one. Any more and she could have suffered some serious damage."

"That s'more was poisoned?" Katy's eyes grew wide.

The doctor nodded.

Darrin rested his arm on her shoulders. "You're lucky. You'll be fine."

"Oh, no. Darrin, someone was trying to poison you."

"We'll discuss this later. We need to get you home for rest and liquids."

Later, in his room reading over the notes of his investigation, so far, he was confused. Though he was suspicious of food and drink, he didn't really expect anything to be wrong. He just believed in erring on the side of caution.

He didn't understand, since he wasn't in a close relationship with any of the women he had met. There wasn't any financial gain for any of them if he were dead. Unlike other victims, he hadn't taken out or signed over any insurance policies, bank accounts, deeds, or married any of the women who pursued him. What would a woman gain from having him dead?

The case had taken a very strange and possibly deadly turn.

CHAPTER 12

Katherine was frightened. Frightened for herself and frightened for Darrin. By having him under her roof, she realized that she was putting herself and her guests in danger. If the suspect poisoned cookies, what would prevent her from poisoning the food and beverages Katherine served for breakfast? She purchased, prepared, and monitored everything she bought and served, but what if there was a weak link and something happened? The scenes running through her mind gave her goose bumps. If not poison, what other devious act did the mystery suspect have up her sleeve? Those detective shows were haunting her.

Damn Darrin. Why did he have to walk into her inn and compromise her safety and the safety of her guests? This was unfair. She was struggling as it is and didn't need any hints of bad publicity to sink her livelihood.

Darrin. Complain as she might, she feared for him. He was the target of a very deranged person. Granted, he put himself in this position by being in law enforcement but he didn't deserve to die for it.

Another care package arrived and the cookies and candy held little appeal. She now viewed everything with suspicion. Poison. Darrin admitted to sending samples off to the lab and trashing the rest. So far, the only poison to be had was found in those mysterious s'mores.

"The s'mores were not made by the bakery," Darrin explained to her. "Someone put them under the dome after they left the bakery. The bakery's goods were not compromised. The delivery boy was innocent. He just picked up the package and delivered it. Somehow while the package was set out for delivery, someone snuck in the poisoned s'mores."

"Who ordered the cookies?" she asked.

"Actually a female minister I had chatted with at the Hall of Philosophy. She checked out as unlikely. She's elderly, as is her husband, and they are highly regarded at the Institution. She was just showing kindness to a stranger. She had called the order into the bakery and never was there in-person. She and her husband do not drive and use scooters on the grounds."

"So, some mystery person tainted the order?"

"Yes," he said.

This was all very strange and unsettling. Darrin seemed as perplexed as she. His concern had grown since the incident and his focus on capturing the suspect had become intense. If this person could poison a batch of s'mores without being caught, what else could she pull off? If she was not after a man's money, what was she after? Who was safe at the Institution? This person was capable of murder and had pharmaceutical experience. Hell, she could poison everyone. When he shared his information with her, Katherine froze.

Ever since, she had a difficult time eating. Unless something was factory sealed or made from scratch by herself, she wasn't eating it or serving it along with bottles, cans, and sealed packages that she personally purchased.

Darrin sat in his room reviewing his notes and the laboratory analysis he had so far. For the first time during his stay, he actually locked the door to his room. Why take chances? Nothing would surprise him after the s'more's incident. What the hell? This was a turn in the investigation he had neither expected nor prepared for.

The thought that Katy could have died weighed heavily on his mind. If she had eaten just one more s'more, she could have been comatose or even worse, dead. As it was, she had fallen ill. She was an innocent victim of his investigation.

Some investigation. Darrin compiled the data he had so far. The suspect was a mystery. Her description differed from interviews with the victim's families. Some described her as blonde, others as a brunette, even a redhead. She was of average height with average features or tall. No one had a photograph of her, as she shied away from cameras and videos. Her name and backstory were different in each case. She apparently obtained her aliases through out of town obituary pages and stole the identities and social security numbers of the deceased.

He pondered the names and causes of death of the six victims. The last victim, number six, was gas lighted with the discontinued anti-depressant Risperine and committed suicide. Number five quickly fell ill and died after drinking a cyanide-laced beverage. The fourth victim drank tea with a morphine-laced derivative. The third was a mystery until an astute coroner found traces of thalium poisoning, a very difficult to trace form of arsenic. The second victim died of kidney failure from a build up of anti-freeze. It was determined that the first victim died from potassium cyanide that was conveniently added to his saltshaker. Over time it built up in his system and killed him. If not for some sharp laboratory work, most of these deaths would have been listed as natural causes.

The killer knew her poisons. She poisoned s'mores, of all the blasted things.

She had to have been a doctor, nurse, or someone in the medical or pharmaceutical field. A normal person would not have her knowledge of complex poisons and their fatal dosages. The woman was brilliant in a deviant, sinister way. She was dangerous. Having her on the prowl at the Institution during the peak of its important Season was a tragedy waiting to happen again.

He went over the list he had composed of the women he had met so far. They all appeared to be typical lonely hearts. He knew that serial killers were sociopaths who often blended in and appeared normal among populations and were difficult to track. They didn't reveal their instability and were outwardly friendly, warm, and caring and appeared harmless.

He determined that this suspect was probably the victim of sexual abuse, hated men, and was out for revenge. Murder probably made her high and happy. The money and property gained was her prize, her trophy. This woman was sitting on over $20 million, so money was not the motive. She had a disdain for wealthy men, though, and made them her target.

There was Mildred the crazy cat lady in her denim and Birkenstocks. She seemed genuinely lonely, was rather unassuming and into quiet pursuits like reading and knitting, instead of adventurous hobbies like most serial killers craved. There was Glenda, the Southern belle with the bad facelift. She was a bit too over-the-top, and most killers didn't purposely bring attention to themselves. The philosophy professor who was into Descartes and Aquinas didn't fit the profile either. Neither did the retired orchestral musician, the retired judge or any of the others he had spent time with. The untainted cookies, pies and cakes were connected to most of these women. If they had wanted to poison him, they had the opportunity. He was beginning to wonder if he even met the woman who poisoned the s'mores. That thought sent a tingle up his spine.

Knowing that someone was out to kill Darrin, and of her being poisoned put Katherine on edge. This was not the summer she had expected. Every time a female guest came and went, she wondered if she were the suspect. When a woman appeared in her lobby, she pondered for a moment the woman's intent. If a package was delivered, she agonized over opening it. If food was delivered, she shoved it away for Darrin to deal with and dispose of. For the first time in years, she despised her job.

As for Darrin, he had been spending more time locked in his room. She suspected that he was conducting research. His social life had quieted and the number of female guests and gifts dwindled as well. For that, she was grateful.

Why couldn't he just be a normal man on vacation? Why did he have to be involved in such sordid and gruesome work? Had he really been Brantley Wentworth, the wealthy software tycoon, they could have been dating and enjoying all of the stimulating discourse and entertainment that the Institution had to offer. It would have been like reliving old times before the fire when they were carefree. Catching up on life would have been better than catching up with a murderer.

"Excuse me," a kittenish voice with a British accent interrupted. Katherine looked up to find a woman standing in front of her counter in the lobby. She wasn't just any woman, but a tall, statuesque blonde with impeccable makeup, coiffed hair in head-to-toe Prada with accessories and jewelry found in Vogue. Her dazzling blue eyes glittered like sapphires. Her age was indecipherable, as she looked like an older version of a fashion doll. She was the most unusual and striking woman Katherine had ever met.

"May I help you?" Katherine stammered.

"Yes, I have been in search of a room, and the Visitor's Center sent me here."

"I should think they would have recommended the Athenaeum." The grand hotel was certainly more this woman's style than a musty old inn.

"This week, the hotel is solidly booked with tours and a big wedding. It serves me right for planning such a last minute trip." The woman smiled. Katherine wondered if her teeth were capped, since they were perfectly straight and white.

"I do have one room available due to a cancellation, but it's rather small and in the garret, third floor. I'm afraid it's a walk up." She noted the woman's high platform Laboutans.

"I'll take it."

Katherine had her sign the guest register and noticed the swirling uphill slant of her signature. Nina Wailson. Interesting name, too.

"I hope you don't mind if I pay with cash. It seems it's all I have at the moment. I just returned from the United Kingdom."

"I see."

After checking her in and depositing the cash in her under-the-counter drop-in safe, she led Miss Wailson up the first of three flights of stairs to her room. The woman wisely removed her shoes and climbed in her bare feet. Being the proprietor, Katherine carried the Vuitton-print suitcase.

At the second floor landing, they were met by a startled Darrin, rather Brantley Wentworth III. Instead of looking at her, Katy observed his complete attention focused toward the new guest. She slunk into the background like the hired help.

"Hi," he said. "Just arriving?"

Nina smiled. "Very observant."

"Here, let me take that." He grabbed the suitcase from Katherine. "Where are you headed?"

"Third floor, garret," Katherine piped in.

"Yikes."

"It's seems to be the only room available this week at the Institution," Nina said, eyes glittering.

"Shall we?" Katherine led them up the next set of stairs to the third floor, where a door led to a very quaint, though very small room with angled ceilings and dormers. It was actually her favorite room. The chintz wallpaper, frilly curtains and country quilt added to its intimacy; the out of the way location, added to its peace and quiet.

"Oh, my, this reminds me of my bedroom in my parents' Yorkshire cottage," Nina said with a giggle.

"You'll feel right at home," Darrin added. "By the way, I'm also a guest here, Brantley Wentworth."

Nina held out her hand and he eagerly grasped it. "Nina Wailson. Pleased to make your acquaintance."

Katherine watched them gaze into each other's eyes and wanted to barf. Was this the same man who kissed her the other night? Was this the man she thought of as the love of her life? Oh, that was Darrin Carter. This was Brantley Wentworth.

"I do hope you find this room acceptable."

"It's absolutely enchanting," Nina said.

"You'll have to excuse me. I have an inn to run." On that note, Katherine turned and rushed down the steps. She couldn't spend another moment with the guest. As she reached the lobby, tears rolled from her eyes.

"I don't care," she assured herself. "What we had was in the past and you cannot go backward, only forward." Now, if only she could believe it.

Darrin wondered if he had lost his mind. Never had a woman he just met set him on fire so fast. If he had been hit over the head with a sledgehammer, he wouldn't have been more surprised. Not only was she physically striking, with that velvet accent, she was intelligent as all hell. After Katy left, they had quite a chat. He even asked her out to dinner that night. After Katy …

Damn. What was Katy to think? He completely forgot about and disregarded her, due to his enchantment over the blonde bombshell. His male hormones had been in overdrive, and it was not a good scene. The last thing he ever wanted to do was hurt Katy. She was special and deserved better treatment.

When he walked into the lobby later that evening, escorting Nina, Katy was at her post. She looked up from the counter and he caught her gaze. There was the sadness of defeat in her eyes. Ignoring them, she looked down at whatever she was doing or pretending to do.

"So, where are we off to for dinner?" Nina asked with a lilt in her voice, casting a glance at Katy.

"Off the grounds, the Watermark. I reserved a table overlooking the lake at dusk."

"Sounds pretty." She grasped his arm.

He led her out of the lobby and into the crisp evening air. What the hell was he doing?

CHAPTER 13

Katherine was out in the backyard of the inn hanging laundry on a clothesline strung between two tall trees. She preferred the sheets to dry outside, where they could catch the fresh scent of the summer air and breezes. She was pinning the second line of sheets, the load in her wicker basket getting lighter. The sheets wafted in the breeze like the sails on the boats out on the lake this sunny early morning.

"I thought that's what dryers are for," Darrin's voice startled her from her work. What did he want? Why wasn't he out on a jog with his blonde Amazon? She had seen Nina leave in her jaunty Capri yoga pants and midriff-baring tee. She ignored him, continuing her chores.

"Hey, I'm sorry about yesterday. I was rude."

Is that what he called it? She continued to ignore him.

"Nina's an interesting person, that's all."

Right. She had nothing to say to him and didn't.

He came around to the front of where she was about to hang a sheet. He grabbed it before she could pin it to form a barrier between them.

"Come on, Katy, I'm a guy and I'm the one who had a lapse in judgement."

She stared right at him. "I really don't care what you do or who you are with. That's your business. This is my business." She grabbed the sheet from him and pinned it to the line, blocking him out.

"Hey." He came around to her side.

"Darrin, we're old friends and a couple of nights ago, I had the lapse in judgment." Yeah, like when she kissed him back.

"We're also partners. You've been helping me on the case."

She spun around to face him. "Helping? Do you call being your royal taste tester helping? I almost died because of your case and your evidence and your … admirers. I'm done helping. Got it?"

He just stared at her.

She grabbed her half empty basket of laundry and stormed toward the back door. Resting it on her knee, she opened the screen door and raced inside. Why didn't he just check out of her inn and find another innkeeper to torment? He could take that perfect blonde with him!

Darrin stood in stunned silence. There was fire burning in her. He was just trying to be apologetic. He shrugged. Royal taste tester? He wasn't the one who made her eat the s'more. She knew good and well that he wasn't eating anything delivered to the inn out of safety concerns. It wasn't his fault that the admirers were suspects.

Could she possibly have feelings for him after all of these years? Did that kiss in the rain the other night mean more than just reliving old times and old feelings?

He smiled. Was she now jealous of some female competition, if that's what she was thinking? He had to admit that he found Nina extremely fascinating. He had never met a woman who was truly a complete package of beauty, charm, sophistication, glamour, breeding, worldliness, education, intelligence, and more. She was also sexy as hell.

They did enjoy a lovely evening sipping wine while watching the sunset over the lake. The cognac-laced lobster bisque and grilled salmon were perfection. Nina was enchanting and never at a loss for words. She seemed to know a little about everything. It seemed that she had inherited funds from her family's trust and traveled the world to experience new people and places. She was told of the Chautauqua Institution and thought that she'd give it a week or more, if she liked it. Crème Brulee was served under the moon and sprinkling of stars.

After returning to the grounds of the Institution, he escorted her on a walk by the lake, inhaling the cool lake breeze. Holding her hand was electric and the night magical. Yet, something was missing.

He couldn't put a handle on it until he was back in his bed at the inn. There was a reason kissing her goodnight didn't seem appropriate or right. For all of her beauty and brains, Nina wasn't Katy.

Through the years, Katy still had a magnetic hold on him. It was something he could not rationalize or explain. No other woman filled his mind with her memories, the experiences they had shared, and the hopes and dreams they had planned. Without her, there was a void in his heart as well.

As he pondered these realizations, the Dragnet ringtone on his smart phone startled him.

"Carter," he answered.

"Sgt. Palmer, Chautauqua Institution Police. There's been a drowning by Heinz Beach. I thought I'd make you aware because of your investigation."

"Shit." Darrin grabbed his pants, polo shirt and slipped on his Sperry's. He raced down South Lake Road to Heinz, where he saw the flashing red lights of the fire department's rescue squad and patrol car. A small crowd of gawkers had congregated.

The sergeant recognized him and let him approach the rescue squad. He waved him inside where he viewed the body. It was of a man, probably in his seventies with white hair attired in khaki, designer polo, and leather sandals. On his wrist was a Rolex watch. Indications showed that the drowning was recent and the body fresh. A sense of foreboding overcame him. The man fit the demographic of the victims. Had the "Siren" struck again? Right under his nose?

"Just happened. Some kids making out near the camp spotted the body, half in the water and half on the beach. He had a faint pulse when we got to him. Even with CPR and AED, he was beyond resuscitating."

"Any witnesses?"

"Just the kids." He pointed out a young couple huddled together near the patrol car. "We questioned them, though they had been a bit too preoccupied to notice what was going on."

"I'll go talk to them, in private."

"I'll get them into the station tomorrow."

"Tonight," Darrin insisted. He wanted to hear their observations while still fresh on their minds. Sleep had a way of altering reality.

"Okay." The sergeant shrugged. "This doesn't make sense. Maybe the guy was drunk."

"That's why I'd like an autopsy as soon as possible and toxicology reports as soon as they are available. This could be a break in my case."

"Or just coincidence?"

"We need to make sure. The safety of guests is on the line. If the "Siren" is here, we need to know and determine her next step before there are more victims."

"You're scaring me. Agent Carter."

"We need to be afraid, very afraid."

The two teenagers were cooperative. Though more concerned about their parents wondering where they were and what they were up to, they willingly talked. Darrin listened carefully, recording the conversation and taking copious notes. They reminded him of Katy and him all those years ago.

"I heard a splash and was startled because it was louder than a wave. Sounded like someone falling off the dock," the boy began.

"I heard it, too, and got a little scared because I thought we were alone," the girl added.

"We quietly walked toward the dock. It was dark and we hid behind bushes, not wanting to be heard or seen," the boy continued. "It was weird. Everything was so quiet after the splash."

"Was anyone else present?" Darrin asked.

"Well, there was a shadow of another person but it ran away, up the hill toward the south and disappeared."

"Like a phantom," the girl added.

"Was this person male or female?"

The teens shrugged.

"Don't know."

"Couldn't tell."

"And then what?" Darrin was getting hyper.

"After the person left, we went over to the dock out of curiosity," the boy said, "And we saw it."

"It?"

"A body floating and the waves were pushing it toward the shore."

"That's when I called 911," the girl said, voice quivering.

"Was the body moving?"

"Moving? It looked dead to me," the boy said.

"And the police came, and then the rescue squad," the girl added.

Darrin walked back to the inn in silence. The evening had taken quite a turn, from a date to a murder. He couldn't say with accuracy that it was indeed a murder but it was suspicious. An older guy out on a dock with another person late at night, when he fell or was pushed into the water. No screaming, no flailing, just silence in the night. The other person runs away as the body floats to shore.

He knew that sleep would be evading him. His mind was racing with anxious anticipation at the autopsy and toxicology reports. He had the gut feeling that this was not an accident. The Season had seven weeks left, plenty of time for more suspicious activity.

The thing that hurt him the most was that he had been unable to out the "Siren." She had to be in his midst. If he only knew where to look.

CHAPTER 14

Katherine had the mind not to talk to Darrin again after their last conversation. The story about a late night drowning at Heinz Beach was spreading like wildfire around the grounds. Knowing about Darrin's case, she couldn't help but wonder if the incident was somehow related. The thought of a serial killer prowling the grounds and preying on guests and residents was putting her on edge.

Darrin ambled down the stairs looking disheveled. His clothes were wrinkled, his hair tussled and he needed a shave. He still looked better than most men she had observed in the morning.

"Look who the cat dragged in," she said, shuffling papers to look busy while seated behind her counter.

"Good morning to you, too," he replied.

"I just put out a fresh pot of strong coffee in the conservatory. You look like you need it."

"A bottle of vodka, too?"

"Bad night?" She assumed it was related to the drowning.

"Very. I don't want to talk about it." He walked toward the glassed-in room, turned and entered.

She shook her head. Of course, he wouldn't.

She looked up just in time to see Nina bopping in from outside. Her slender figure was accented by basic black yoga togs, and she carried a purple yoga mat.

"Morning," she greeted in a cheerful voice, and flashed her perfect smile.

"Have fun?" Katherine asked, as if she cared.

"Nothing like a good stretch to start the morning. I absolutely am addicted to yoga. Ever try it?"

"I don't have the time."

"That's really too bad." Nina smiled again, and headed toward the conservatory. How lucky for her since Darrin, rather Brantley was in there. Maybe he'd charm her.

Katherine shuffled more papers out of nervous habit. She really hadn't much paperwork. Though she really didn't need to sit at her counter in the lobby all day, she did. Part of it was pride in being an innkeeper and keeping watch over her investment. Part of it was to be available if a guest needed assistance, or if someone requested reservations. Most innkeepers sat at their front desks only in the morning, in case guests had any questions from the evening before or had issues with their accommodations that needed addressing. They stayed at their posts all day only on Saturdays when guests checked out and new guests checked in.

She wouldn't admit that she stayed at her post because it was safe. She had an excuse not to venture out and experience the Institution's grounds during the Season. Seeing the visitors so carefree and happy made her sad. Memories were conjured up making her confront her past and face all that she had lost. Staying inside kept the memories contained. Except for trips to the post office, she rarely walked the grounds. Her only escape was in her car, which was parked behind the inn, that she would use to go into Mayville for groceries, to the hardware store or to run other errands. Her life had been relegated to being wallpaper, a small part of the tapestry that was the Chautauqua Institution.

Mildred walked into the lobby. The gray bob, Birkenstock sandals with socks lady. Today, she was attired in a bright floral print shirtdress, a departure from the scholarly-preppie look.

"Morning," Mildred said, approaching the counter. She handed Katherine the hardback book she had been holding. "Could you get this to Mr. Wentworth? It's a discourse on crime and punishment. We had quite an interesting discussion the other day. I thought that he'd like to borrow it."

Katherine took the book. "I'll be sure that he gets it."

"Could you tell him that we'll have to meet for lunch to discuss it?"

"Of course. I'll tell him."

"Thank you."

Mildred turned and left.

Katherine looked at the book, another article for Darrin. At least this one wasn't edible and it did pertain to his secret line of work. Mildred. She was about as opposite from Darrin as night was from day. She could have easily been his mother. Most of the women who pursued him were, except for Nina. Nina. She was the exception, especially at the Institution where Hollywood glamour was not the norm. It was no wonder that Darrin found her attractive and interesting. Katherine wanted to gag.

About an hour had passed when Darrin and Nina emerged from the conservatory, laughing. He was carrying the yoga mat, while Nina entertained him with animated arm movements and conversation. She was as elegant as a swan and fluid as a dancer. Katherine observed them as she slunk into her seat, shrinking in significance. How could a man like Darrin resist someone so alive?

"I need to get tidied up and changed," Nina was overheard saying.

Darrin smiled. "And I have to check my business correspondence."

"You know what they say, all work and no play makes you a dull boy." Nina winked and scurried upstairs.

Darrin shook his head and shoved his hands into his shorts' pockets.

"Someone is in a better mood," Katherine said.

"The coffee helped."

"And something, well, someone?" She smirked.

"Come on, Katy, Nina is a fun lady and we had a delightful chat. She takes my mind off of the case."

"So, how's it going?"

"I really can't discuss it. Let's just say that things are a bit tense."

"The drowning last night have anything to do with it?" She stared at him to gauge his reaction and wasn't disappointed. He'd make a lousy poker player. His eyes lit up and he tensed.

"What did you hear about it?"

"Only that some older guy drowned last night. There's plenty of speculation but authorities seem to be treating it as an accident, at least that's what's being spread around the grounds."

"That's good." He sighed and she took it as a sign of relief.

He turned to leave.

She stopped him. "Oh, before I forget. Mildred dropped this off for you."

She handed him the book and he accepted it.

"Mildred?" For a moment he looked confused. "Oh, Mildred."

"One of your fans."

"She's quite a character. She acts all prim and proper and low key but behind those glasses is a seductress."

"Hmmm, suspect material?"

"I am not ruling anyone out."

"I guess I'll have to mind my P's and Q's." She laughed.

He pointed a finger at her, chuckling, “Even you.” He walked away toward he stairs and looking back, “I have a lot of work to do.”

CHAPTER 15

A lot of work was an understatement. It was more like a deluge. When Darrin checked his cell while having coffee, he noted a text from the coroner in Erie. The autopsy had been conducted overnight and samples taken for and sent to the crime lab. Though anxious to get the results, Nina had walked in and made herself comfortable at his table. Having her join him for coffee was actually a welcome diversion and a pleasant start to the day. He knew that his mood would go downhill from there. Investigating a murder was serious and emotionally draining. Some agents were able to disconnect more easily from the victims and the crimes. From outward appearance, he seemed as analytical and unaffected. Deep inside, though, he harbored sensitivity. To his credit, he knew that this quality is what motivated him to pursue justice for the deceased and their families. He viewed each victim as a member of his family and their family as his family. It put things into perspective. So far in his career it had paid off. His intent was to doggedly investigate this case with the same junkyard dog determination.

In the privacy of his suite, he checked his e-mail and opened the attached coroner's report, complete with documentary photographs. He lay back in his bed resting his head against a pillow and the headboard with the laptop on his lap. Scrolling through the information, the autopsy details were revealed step by gory step.

One detail caught his attention and he had to go over it several times. Though the body had shown no blunt force trauma or any trauma for that matter, there was a suspicious needle mark on the subject's neck, at the jugular vein. The coroner's office had highlighted it.

Even drug addicts did not normally inject drugs at the neck, so it was unlikely that an older, sophisticated gentleman would do so. Most likely, someone jabbed him with a needle the evening of the drowning, as the mark was fresh.

The mystery was what drug was injected into his system and whether it caused him to pass out and drown. The toxicology report, promised to be rushed in a few days, would reveal all.

In the meantime, Darrin needed to learn more about the victim. From the wallet the man still had in his pocket upon his death, it was learned that his name was Kenneth Spotzworthy from Denver, Colorado. From the black metal American Express card, he seemed rather well off. If it was murder, the motive certainly wasn't robbery.

Phone calls were made to the next of kin, in this case his married son and single daughter. Their father spent every summer at the Institution, as he had with their mother who had died of breast cancer less than a year ago. Their father was lonely without his wife but decided to rent the same condo on the grounds for the familiarity and the memories.

His family was unaware of any relationships or female companions, as their father still seemed to be in a state of grief. He had been a retired contractor who had sold his business to a conglomerate for a tidy sum. Of course, they were shattered to hear of their father's untimely and shocking demise.

Darrin looked at the man's face as he lay on the gurney in the forensic photographs and knew how unfair it was. This handsome, refined man deserved a longer life with the love of his children, grandchildren and a woman who could have loved him. He didn't deserve to die in a place deemed safe in such a sinister manner. Darrin vowed to find the murderer, whatever it took.

Katherine was on edge. The summer was taking quite a turn. First, it was Darrin's shocking reappearance into her life, and now a mystery murderer prowling the grounds.

Both were dangerous.

She stood by the stainless kitchen sink, rinsing and loading the dishwasher after morning breakfast. Not a scrap of food remained on any plates. Apparently the cinnamon buns, fruit tart, and French toast were a hit with her guests. There weren't any leftovers either. Hers was one of the few inns on the grounds that served a complementary breakfast to guests, and she took pride in that fact. It also made people feel comfortable and at home. Breakfast in the conservatory also introduced them to one another, and many friendships had been forged and even one or two romances.

Romance? That was the last thing she wanted to think about. Her thoughts always drifted to Darrin and their past. That was the past, she had to keep reminding herself. One kiss did not create a future. That was obvious with Darrin's interest in Nina.

The bell on the lobby counter rang. Someone needed assistance. It was always while she was away from her post. She pulled off her apron, smoothed the creases in her slacks and rushed out into the lobby. The sight of the slender, tanned blonde with the turned up nose, pouty lips and arrogant demeanor made her freeze in her tracks.

"Aunt Agatha?" She met the woman's steely gray gaze.

"Yes, Katherine, it's your auntie come to visit," the woman replied in a gruff tone in a smoky voice that was all too familiar.

Aunt Aggie was her father's younger sister who had taken her in after her parents died. The aunt who treated her more like a charity case than a relative. The aunt who turned her out at eighteen to fend for herself. What the hell was the bitch doing in Chautauqua? She was sure she'd have her answer soon enough. If seeing Darrin was a shock, this was even more unexpected.

"What a surprise. What brings you here?"

"Opportunity and the inn."

Katherine stared at her. What business would the woman in head-to-toe Escada, sitting on an estate worth a cool $14 million want at the inn? The woman was cold and heartless, just as her father had been, and an opportunist.

"Really?"

"I want to take it off your hands and will pay you handsomely for the privilege."

Her aunt was a person who always got to the point. She always got her way but would not this time.

"It's not for sale," Katherine said matter-of-factly.

"It can be. Just look around. This place is a dump. It's also tainted. It should be shut down and torn down." She pointed to the walls with faded paper and the scuffed floors.

"I don't need your advice or your money."

"Not from what my accountant says."

"You and your accountant have no business prying into my affairs. This is my inn, my home and it's remaining that way." Her heart was racing and her breathing turned into seething.

"You can work for me, in my hotel. You'd make more money for less work."

Hell would freeze over before she had anything to do with Aggie. This was the woman who treated her like a scullery maid, her own children like royalty. She had done enough housework to earn her keep growing up, and she was damned if she would do so as an adult. Her hotel?

"What hotel?"

"The lake lot I'm purchasing and building the most modern facility on the grounds. I have the permits and contractor."

She placed her hands on her hips to keep them from shaking, and to prevent the urge from punching her. It was widely known that there was a lakefront lot for sale on North Lake."

Aggie must be bored, Katherine thought. Didn't she just lose her ... What was it? Third husband? Or was it her fourth? The woman always married wealthy older men with health issues and each died of some weird malady. Maybe she came to Chautauqua to meet her next husband and conquest. She wouldn't put it past her.

"I'll make you interested." It sounded like a threat. "You'd be a better employee than owner. Face it, mental illness runs in your mother's family. You just aren't capable of making this place a success. Besides, it's not a real inn but a dilapidated old fixer-upper."

"It's best that you leave the premises," Katherine said. "I don't have any rooms for rent and even if I did, I wouldn't have any available for you."

Her aunt chuckled, shaking her head. "Do you honestly think I'd stay in this hovel? It would have to be rebuilt up to my standards before I'd spend a night here."

"I have work to do." Katherine turned and began to walk away.

"So do I," her aunt replied in a sinister tone that Katherine found unnerving.

The woman left, slamming the screen door behind.

"What the hell is going on?" Katherine asked out loud.

CHAPTER 16

Phenobarbital. Kenneth Spotzworthy, the drowning victim had been injected with the substance before he fell or was pushed off the dock. Why was Darrin not surprised? The suspect had a vendetta.

"Hell hath no fury like a woman scorned."

Darrin decided to relieve pent-up tension, as he always had, by working out. He hadn't seen the inside of a gym since leaving Manhattan. He walked down South Lake Road to Heinz Fitness Center, located on the same beach where the body had been discovered the other night. Goosebumps crept up his arms.

Turning away from the lake and docks, he walked up the curving ramp to the entrance, paid the fee and hopped on a treadmill. Walking the scenic grounds wouldn't have afforded the fast pace and free mind the machine offered. Seeing landmarks on the grounds would have only brought back repressed memories and the case. Plugging his ear buds into his I-Pod, he hoped that vintage Rolling Stones would drown out his thoughts for a while.

Damp with perspiration, he left Heinz. A dip in the lake seemed like a great idea until visions of a cold alabaster body of an elderly male changed his mind. As he turned to leave, a figure climbing up a ladder from the dock caught his eye.

Nina emerged from the lake like a sea nymph. Her bare skin glistened in the sunlight, her hair plastered away from her face, her sculpted body barely contained in a red string bikini. She was a sight to behold. His body reacted before his mind. Thank goodness for the baggy cargo shorts. Their eyes met. Strangely, he found her gaze to be devoid of warmth. Though her smile was welcoming enough, something wasn't right.

He waved and she waved back. Hesitating, he watched her step onto the dock. She grabbed a towel and swiped her body as she walked toward him, beige aqua shoes on her feet. Smart girl, he thought. She heeded the signs about small stones and sharp shells on the lake bottom.

"Hi." She flung the towel over her shoulder.

"Hi," he said, noting the rise of her ample bosom in the skimpy halter.

"Finally, it's been warm enough for a swim." Her accent was lilting.

"Finally."

"You could use some cooling off." She winked.

"Oh?" He looked down, realizing that his damp tee shirt was the reason for her comment. "I'm not in the mood."

He wondered if she knew about the body on the beach. She appeared so unaffected. He wouldn't tell her that a drowning victim made him dislike the idea of swimming in the lake. No use ruining her fun.

"Do you swim?"

He shoved his hands in his pants' pocket. "Actually, I was on my high school swim team."

"Interesting. Then again, you are such an interesting person." She smiled.

What the heck was wrong with him? This beautiful, flirtatious woman should have been welcome company. Yet, every time he was with her, all he could think of was Katy. Katy, whose eyes were warm and welcoming. Katy who was young and beautiful in a wholesome way. Katy with the soft lips.

"Brantley, how about we grab a bite tonight after you escort me back to the inn?" she asked.

For a moment, he paused. Responding to the name Brantley was still uncomfortable.

"I'll walk you to the inn but I have office work to catch up on so I'm afraid dinner won't work."

"You'll still have to eat."

"Sorry, Nina, I really can't."

She grimaced, her smile fading. Apparently few men turned her down, he surmised.

"I'll grab my things," she said in a curt tone, abruptly turning to scoop up her tote. She pulled a flowing caftan over her suit.

They walked up South Lake Road in silence. Darrin thought it strange how one rejection could turn her cool and quiet.

When a South tram drove by, she flagged the driver. Without a word, she stepped on board. Instead of joining her, he waved she and the bus on.

"I don't need the distraction," he muttered aloud. As if Katy wasn't enough.

Katherine was spray cleaning the front windows inside when Nina came charging in. It was the first time she witnessed the woman rattled and unsmiling. Nina didn't acknowledge her but proceeded up the stairs, two at a time, to her room. Katherine just shook her head, continuing the task at hand.

When Darrin entered the lobby, he was pensive, ignoring her until he caught himself and turned to face her.

"Oh, oh, lover's quarrel?" Katherine asked.

"What?" His eyes narrowed.

"Just wondering. Nina looked upset, so I thought …"

"Trouble is, Katy, you think too much. Nina asked me out to dinner, and I declined her invitation."

"You have a strange effect on women." She sprayed the glass and wiped it.

"It's weird how upset she got." He shook his head. "I hardly know the woman."

"Apparently, she'd like to get to know you better, Mr. Wentworth."

"I don't know myself anymore."

"Must be multiple personality disorder." She laughed. "I don't think Nina's a woman who's used to getting turned down and not getting her way, as in high-maintenance."

He smirked. "Most women are."

"You think?"

"And you?"

"Try no maintenance."

"Whatever you're doing, you're doing right." His gaze sized her up from head to toe.

Hearing a compliment from Darrin was going to turn her back into a blushing schoolgirl. "You don't have to pander to me."

"Just accept the compliment and say thank you." He smiled. She almost forgot about his cute dimples, the way his lip turned up Elvis-style, and the how his eyes sparkled when he smiled.

"Thank you." She met his gaze and felt fifteen again. If time could only be turned back and life lived over, where would they be?

He sighed. "Being back makes me wonder where our paths would have taken us if not for the fire."

The jolt of him having the same thoughts as she, made her quiver. She stepped away from the window and walked to the counter, setting the spray bottle and rag on top.

He followed her.

"You have the same thoughts, don't you?"

She nodded. "The past is over and done." She went behind the counter, putting the space between them.

"But the present is a gift."

"Someone spends too much time on Facebook, with all of those inspiring aphorisms."

He chuckled. "And you are hiding behind that counter again."

"What?"

"Face it, that counter has become your security blanket."

"Crazy."

He leaned against the wood. "Remember, my background is in behavioral science."

"Well, you don't need to psychoanalyze me." His words made her tremble, and admit that he was right. Behind the counter she was safe and in control. It suited the proprietor of an inn. Away from the inn, she was vulnerable, exposed and not in charge.

"What are you afraid of?"

"In my business, you have no time to be afraid." She scoffed.

"Oh, but you are. Away from your counter, you're on edge. I've seen how you tremble and fidget and look around as if someone might be after you. The ghosts of the past are not going to haunt you."

He was touching a raw nerve. She reached for her ledger, blindly opened it and pretended to review names.

Before she could act, he reached over and slammed the leather-bound journal closed.

"You may escape from most people, Katy, but you can't run away from me. I know you all too well."

"No! You knew the fifteen-year-old girl. You don't know the adult woman. You haven't been a part of my life for years to even begin to understand me."

"Time may change physical appearance but the essence of the person is still the same."

"Don't you have anything better to do than harass me?" She was flustered. He was delving into her mind and she didn't like it.

"The truth hurts. Hey, I didn't escape from the past unscathed."

"Other than choosing a career in law enforcement, you don't seem affected."

"Just like you, my scars don't show. The mental as well as the physical."

She swallowed hard. The fire had left a lasting imprint on them. They had both inhaled deadly smoke and had suffered burns. There was a reason for her not wearing a swimsuit and being careful with wardrobe choices. She had to admit it was the reason she refused to undress in front of anyone. Her imperfect body impacted her sex life. Men sought perfection. Apparently, he had issues as well. Being a woman, she assumed that her altered appearance was more pronounced and more difficult to deal with.

"You can't hide scars forever," he said in an all-too-serious tone.

She shifted on her feet. "This isn't fair. Why are you interrogating me?"

"Maybe because I still care for you?"

Before she could digest his words, Mildred popped into the lobby.

"Afternoon," she chirped. "Brantley, you're just the person I wanted to see."

Katherine noticed how he rolled his eyes before turning to face the plain woman with the rainbow-hued toe socks slipped into her Birkenstocks.

"Hi Mildred," he greeted with a forced smile.

"How did you like the book?" she asked with a crooked grin.

"Book"

"The treatise?"

"Oh, that book. I'll tell you, I have been so busy working, I haven't had the time to get to it."

Mildred squinted while her eyes formed a thin line. "Do you think you'll ever get to it?"

Katherine observed yet another woman growing peeved, all over a damned book.

"I was really looking forward to your insights." Mildred said, her face growing flush.

Darrin shrugged. "The best I can do is try."

"Then, try." Mildred abruptly turned and marched out of the inn.

"You have a strange effect on women," Katherine said.

"Yeah, pissing them off."

"Is that your preferred method of nabbing a suspect?"

CHAPTER 17

Everything about her was fake. She seemed like the perfect suspect candidate, Darrin thought. That evening he decided to try the wine and tapas Happy Hour at the Heirloom Restaurant at the Athenaeum Hotel. Balancing a glass of Riesling in one hand and a plate of Mediterranean chips and dip in the other, he was knocked off balance by a slim, tan blonde with fluffy blonde hair and piercing gray eyes.

"Excuse me," she apologized in a smoky voice.

She had her hands full with a glass of red wine, and a salad plate. Her smile was effervescent. Darrin surmised that her perfect teeth were capped, her face altered to appear younger than her hands revealed, and her fit figure honed by exercise and a surgeon's adept sculpting. Her attire was preppy Lily Pulitzer. He hadn't seen her on the grounds.

"I guess I was in too much of a hurry to grab a seat on the veranda," she said.

"That's okay, it was my plan, too." He smiled to be friendly.

They walked to the door way and he motioned with a tilt of his head, "After you."

She sashayed through the doorway and to a table with an unobstructed view of the lake. She sat, and motioned for him to join her and set down her plate. He sat across from her and set his plate down as well.

Glancing around, she said, "It looks like Noah's Ark out here. Everyone is in tables of two. I thought that we should do the same … that is, if you're alone, as am I."

Was she flirting? He told himself that this was business and she was just a new suspect. "I'm alone."

"Agatha Cromwell," she introduced, offering her hand. "Friends call me Aggie."

"Brantley Wentworth III," he introduced, shaking her hand. She had a firm grip.

"What happened to the other two?" She laughed, fingering her hair.

"Huh?"

"Just teasing. You said that you were the third." Her eyes sparkled.

"Just stuck with the lineage."

"Where are you from?"

"California. Silicon Valley."

"You don't strike me as being a computer geek."

"Trust me, I'm as geeky as they get." He just hoped that she wasn't into computers, hardware or software design. He may have had the cover but not the experience. His knowledge of computers was consumer-level at best.

"I'm as non-Geek as they get. I don't even own a computer." She laughed in a deep throaty way.

Saved. She didn't know computers.

"Where are you from?" he asked.

"Connecticut."

"On vacation?"

"Investing," she said. "I just bought some property, where I plan to build the most modern hotel at the Institution."

Another innkeeper? He just left one, Katy. "Is that so? I didn't think modern was allowed."

"It's north, and not in the historic district. Besides, it will keep with the Victorian theme but be state-of-the-art. There are too many musty old buildings around here. I'm sure there are people who prefer real five-star accommodations."

"I guess you have a point. Where are you staying?"

"Here. It's not five-star," she said with a bite in her voice. "I guess it's the best there is at the moment."

"The food's good." He dipped into his plate.

"It'll do. So where are you staying, Bill Gate's competitor?" She met his gaze. Another hollow soul, he thought with one look into her eyes.

"At the Honeysuckle Inn."

"Yuck. You could do better than that. That place is the worst there is."

"I think it's rather quaint."

"Do you know its history?"

Play dumb. "Not much."

"It was a family home until a tragedy spoiled it. It's haunted. A crazy woman slit her wrists in one of the bathrooms. Her mentally unstable daughter runs the place. I'd lock my door at night in that place." She was cool and stoic.

He knew that Katy's mother had committed suicide but didn't know all of the details. Swallowing hard, he never considered Katy mentally unstable.

"Do you know the family?"

"Yes. Nut cases." She shook her head. "Let's talk about more pleasant things." She changed the subject.

A familiar voice jolted him from his thoughts and their conversation.

"I see that you came out to eat after all." The British accent had a bite to it.

He looked up to meet Nina's fiery gaze. She held a glass of white wine and a plate of fried calamari.

"I finished my work early."

"I see." She stared a hole through Agatha.

"You could join us, dear, if you'd like," Agatha offered in a condescending manner.

"I'd rather dine alone." Nina's eyes burned with fire as they met Darrin's. She turned abruptly and walked across the veranda to a far away table.

"Jealous girlfriend?" Agatha laughed.

"Just an acquaintance."

"Looks to me that she'd like to be more."

He sighed.

"Must be difficult being a man around here," she said, after sipping her wine.

"Why?"

"It seems to me that men are hunted like wild game with all these single women vying for a trophy."

She was right and having her admit it made him wonder about her motives.

"You aren't seeking a trophy?" he asked.

"I have enough trophies on my shelf." She winked.

He believed it by her looks, manner, and the quality gold and diamond jewelry she wore. Aggie needed further investigating.

Katherine had moved from her counter to the dining room. In the late evening, it was devoid of guests. The dining room was also one of the few rooms in the house that held pleasant memories. Memories of dinner with her parents and grandparents lingered in the ornate Victorian space. The original wall covering was faded, though elegant, the wood blinds chipped but operational and the summer curtains light and airy. The massive carved buffet was set with her ancestor's sterling tea set, the sideboard with their gilt rimmed china. She sat at the heavy mahogany table in an ornately carved leather upholstered chair. An antique lace tablecloth draped the table with a sterling epergne set atop a mirrored plateau.

She spread out her bills and flipped open her laptop. The spreadsheet application was open. There was nothing more disheartening than to see where her income was being spent. So far, she was barely breaking even. At least she wasn't in the red.

The creak of the front door opening interrupted her thoughts. A guest was probably coming in from a late-night stroll. She had grown accustomed to guests filtering in at all hours. Though the quiet-time curfew was 11 p.m., people could come and go at all hours. The sound, though, always unnerved her. She wished that she could just lock the door at midnight and be done with it. With the recent crimes, she was even more on edge.

With a sigh, she left the spreadsheet application and checked e-mails. The posts she enjoyed the most were from the Chautauqua Grapevine, an informal e-mail loop primarily used by full-time and Seasonal residents. She found the news and gossip entertaining. There were the lost and found items, gripes, and complaints and concerns.

She reviewed posts pertaining to her aunt's recent land acquisition. Aunt Aggie sure knew how to stir up controversy. Residents were not happy with her purchase of prime North Lake property for an inn, preferring the property remain residential. She was also hiring a renowned architect from New York City to design her modern facility. The word "contemporary" in and of itself was enough to send old-timer's blood to boiling. Aggie also had the audacity to request a variance to construct a ten-story structure. Luckily, even her money and donations to the Chautauqua Fund couldn't buy her that request. Blocking the lake view of residents across the road was not permitted. Adding to the controversy, was that Aggie had never stayed, rented, or resided at the Institution. Aggie may have known how to influence people, but she certainly didn't know how to win friends.

Why her aunt would show up at the Institution to cause trouble was beyond her. The woman could have chosen any resort town in the country to apply her ideas and her money. Why did she have to do it at the Institution? Did her aunt still hate her after all of these years? Did her aunt want to somehow exact revenge on her mother's family and memory through her?

Aunt Agatha had always blamed the fire on her mother. She could not accept the fact that her father was at fault. Aggie's brother and his mistress caused the fatal fire. Yet, Agatha still held the belief that her mother somehow lit the flames and caused the death and destruction, though it had been proven that her mother had committed suicide prior to the fire. Katy had witnessed it. Her aunt wanted to ignore the fact that Katy found her mother's body and rushed to the inn to witness her father go up in flames. She wanted to ignore the fact that there was a mistress involved and a lover's quarrel.

Agatha had idolized her brother. With his movie-star good looks, charm, and Ivy League education and manner, he could do no wrong. To her, he was far too perfect for any woman. She wouldn't have approved of any woman he married. Her mother wasn't going to be accepted, no matter who she was.

None of Aggie's husbands could stack up either. She kept searching for a man to be a likeness of her beloved brother. When a husband failed to live up to her expectations, she divorced him or he died from living with her wrath.

When her brother died, Aggie was beside herself. Her only sibling was gone. The love of her life was gone. She wouldn't accept it back then and, apparently, couldn't accept it now. How weird and perverted, Katy thought. What a sad way to live one's life.

The scream from upstairs was ear-piercing and echoed off the walls of the inn, jolting her from her seat. It was as bloodcurdling as that from a Halloween horror movie, and she flinched. Shivers curled up her spine and she trembled. There was a loud thump. Footsteps scurrying about pounded and creaked the upper floorboards. Panicked voices and additional screams added to her fear. She jumped up from her seat.

Being her inn, she was responsible for whatever happened, good and bad. She forced her legs to move and she bolted up the stairs to the second floor where a crowd had gathered outside a guest room. The door was open. As she approached she could see the body of a man, face down on the floor, a wood cane nearby. She instantly knew who it was. The very dapper Forrest Anderson had been a regular every Season since the inn opened. A retired college professor, English Literature, he had the manner of a country gentleman.

Pushing her way through the gathered guests, she entered the room.

"Don't come any closer," Darrin warned, looking up from his kneeling position at the man's side. "The police have been called. We don't want to disturb any evidence."

She could sense his fear and concern and her heart began to beat wildly.

"What … What happened?" she asked.

"Heart attack," he replied, though the tone of his voice revealed it was something more. "Can you get everyone back in their rooms?"

"Okay, the police and EMS have been called. Everything's going to be okay," Katherine assured the crowd, trying her best to be calm and reassuring. "Just go back to your rooms. There's nothing any of us can do tonight."

The guests, most attired in their nightclothes, wandered back to their rooms with hushed whispers. Just when the crowd had dispersed, Nina Wailson came ambling down from her third-floor garret.

"I heard screams. Is everything all right?" she asked with a yawn.

"Everything's fine. A guest just had a heart attack and someone screamed when they saw him. Authorities have been called. Just go back to bed."

"Oh, my. How sad. Good night." Nina turned and went back upstairs.

Katherine waited to make sure that everyone was back in their rooms before stepping into the doorway and whispering to Darrin, "What's going on?"

He pulled the man up by his shirt and she could see the pool of blood beneath his body. She covered her mouth to squelch a scream and the onset of nausea.

"Is he … ?

Before she could finish her question, he nodded.

Police and rescue personnel bounded up the steps. Darrin flashed his F.B.I badge.

"We'll talk, later," Darrin told her. "Just stay in the parlor. We'll need to ask you some questions."

"Okay." She was actually glad to be leaving the grisly scene.

A murder had taken place in her inn! This investigation was too close for comfort. She had to grasp the banister to get downstairs without tripping. Her nerves were fraying and on edge. Who would want to murder that kindly old man? Duh! A woman with killing on her agenda.

She grabbed her laptop from the dining room and went into her parlor, settling on the low, plush settee. Setting the laptop on an end table, she kept it closed. With her legs curled beneath her, she crossed her arms to stop her shaking. Drawing a deep breath, the scent of stargazer lilies from the table reminded her of a funeral home. Nausea once again crept up. She closed her eyes, wanting to escape from the scene.

Police and Sheriff's deputies arrived to secure the crime scene, and the medical examiner and the country's chief of detectives came to take photographs and to gather and preserve evidence.

After what seemed like hours, the body was removed on a stretcher, encased in a black body bag. EMS and police escorted it out of the inn. When they left, Darrin ambled in to the parlor. His face was drawn and hair disheveled. In his hand he carried a digital tape recorder.

He sat on the settee next to her. She was too drained to even notice or care how close he had positioned himself.

"I'm sorry that this had to happen here, of all places," he said in a soft, consoling tone.

She shrugged. "Just my luck. Story of my life."

"I want you to know that this is an unusual case and we're trying to gather evidence thoroughly, yet quickly. It cannot appear to be a murder investigation. No yellow tape. No lengthy disruption. It would be prudent to lets guests believe that he died of a heart attack, a pretty common occurrence on the grounds. To get things back to normal as soon as possible, a crew will be out shortly clean the room and put things in order before daybreak. The police will be in contact with Mr. Anderson's family."

"I understand."

He placed his hand on her arm. "You're trembling."

"Yeah, I wonder why."

"I'm here. You'll be protected." He gave her arm a reassuring squeeze, though she wasn't reassured.

"Are any of us really protected?"

He released her arm. "I have to play cop now since I'm leading this investigation. I'd like to ask you some questions."

"I figured as much." She pointed out the recorder.

"So I get the facts straight when I write my report." He became very serious. "Tell me about Mr. Anderson."

She told him all she knew about the widower from New Hampshire. As long as he'd been coming to the Institution he had been single, alone and seemed to prefer it that way.

No, he never had guests or female companions from what she could tell. He seemed to be in perpetual grief for a wife he had lost so many years before. No, he didn't have children, just a couple of elderly siblings. He was a bit of a loner.

"Did you notice anything unusual tonight?"

She pondered for a moment before answering. "It's not really unusual but shortly before I heard the scream, someone entered the front door and went upstairs?"

"Mr. Anderson?"

"I don't know. I was in the dining room working on my computer and couldn't see anyone. You must understand that it's not unusual for guests to come and go at all hours of the night."

"I definitely understand." Of course, he would.

"Was the scream male or female?"

"I … I don't know. I want to say female as it seemed to register rather high."

"Any other noises?"

"A loud thump."

"Other noises?"

"Just footsteps, voices and some cries. That's when I ran upstairs and found the crowd, you, and the body. I figured you heard everything I heard since you were quickly on the scene."

"I did, and rushed to his room to find him dead. Securing the scene was my next order of business. I just need your witness account since I can't drill the guests without raising their suspicions, though police have made routine inquiries."

"As if the guests don't know something's up?" She shrugged.

"Prior to the scream, was there any noise? A scuffle or a struggle?"

She shook her head, "No. I didn't hear any."

"I gather you still have your supersonic hearing?" He smiled, lips quivering.

In their youth, he used to tease her about her acute hearing. She could hear a wristwatch ticking. Appliance humming and fluorescent lights drove her crazy.

"I still have great hearing."

"Anything else unusual?"

She gave it some thought. "No. Nothing unusual at all."

He clicked off the recorder.

"The only thing unusual is this case and the suspect." He audibly sighed.

"How many people will have to die here before this person is caught?"

"Hopefully, no more. It's perplexing. Previous victims met the murderer here but were killed in their respective states, about one per year. The murderer would only kill after marrying the victim or being named in a will. This Season, two men have been murdered on the premises within two weeks and the murderer hasn't reaped any financial gain."

"Do you think she knows that you're here investigating?"

"I've pondered the cat and mouse theory but it doesn't add up. Her motive seems to have changed."

"She doesn't need the money but still wants the entertainment?"

"Or she wants to be caught?"

"In that case, catching her should be easier."

"I doubt it."

"Do we all have to go about our business watching our back?"

"Yes. Be observant. Be careful. I don't want anything happening to you."

"I'm female. I think that you should be the one worrying."

CHAPTER 18

After interviewing Katy, Darrin went back to his room, down the hall from the latest victim's. He passed the crew in the hall that specialized in cleaning and sanitizing crime scenes after evidence had been gathered, and investigators left. There were jobs more morbid than his.

He couldn't fathom how a murder could have occurred literally right under his nose. He was in his room down the hall working on his laptop when he heard the scream. He had grabbed his semi-automatic pistol, cocked it, and placed it in his pants' pocket as a precaution as he rushed into the hall. Seeing the guest room door ajar, he pushed it slightly with his foot. He entered with caution, hand on the trigger as he swept the perimeter of the room. Assured he was alone, he knelt by the victim, checking his pulse. The body was warm but the victim was dead. Lifting the body by its shirt, he discovered the blood, gaping wound, and the butcher knife beneath the body.

The man had been dressed in street clothes, not in pajamas, as the late hour of night would have suggested. His may have been the footsteps Katy heard entering the inn. The crime scene was fresh. He surmised he had missed seeing the murderer by seconds.

At that moment, the guests showed up with concern and fear. Not revealing his cover, he acted like another guest who just happened to arrive on the scene. Death always brought an audience. Yet, there were no witnesses. No one had heard or seen anything unusual.

Apparently, the man had been stabbed so quickly, and brutally that he never had time to react. A knife to the heart meant instant death. From talking with other guests, the falsetto scream must have been the man's in the throes of death. There were no sounds of fleeing footsteps, just a thump, most probably the man falling to the floor. No furniture was displaced and there was no trail of blood.

He'd dreaded the moment when Katy would arrive on the scene. She had endured enough tragedy in her life. The last thing she needed was more.

When she walked in the doorway, her eyes were wide with fear and her lips parted, as if mortified. Her life was her inn and he hated to break the news of another tragedy, and how it could impact her livelihood.

She was calm in answering his questions, though he knew how rattled she was, as well she should. This murder occurred on her premises with her only a floor below. Two murders and the Season had just begun.

The challenge was to find the suspect before she struck again. The way things were going, the question wasn't if, but when.

When he analyzed the findings from the forensics lab, he was perplexed. The cause of death was the obvious, a knife to the heart. There was an absence of drugs or medications in the man's system, which set this case apart from the previous. The suspect also revealed her cunning. There were no prints on the knife or any surface, no fibers or hair samples and no blood spatter. She was not only precise with a knife, she knew how to cover her tracks.

The knife. At his request, Katy had inventoried her kitchen knives. The murder weapon had been removed from her wood knife block. The news upset her further. Someone had entered her kitchen, taken the knife, cleaned it, and used it to commit a heinous crime. The thought of a murderer lurking in her kitchen made her even more uneasy, which was understandable. The case was getting too close. Even he, as a guest, was set on edge. His suspect not only had entered the inn where he was staying, she stole a knife, and murdered a fellow guest.

When he went downstairs for his morning coffee, he saw Katy perched by her counter. She was engrossed in reading *The Chautauquan Daily* newspaper. He knew that there was no mention of the murder. Just as the drowning by the lake, it was kept quiet. For all intents and purposes, Mr. Anderson died of a massive heart attack.

"Morning," he greeted.

She looked up, lowering the paper. As he approached, she neatly folded it and set it on the counter.

"Morning to you, too," she replied. "I caved in and bought a large lemon tart from Herb Keyser. You'd better grab a piece before it's gone."

"I'll do that." The thought of eating anything at the inn made him uneasy, though he heard about the famous tarts, a fundraiser for the Institution's Annual Fund, and presumed them safe.

"Actually, you're the first guest to come down, so you have it all to yourself."

"Lucky me. That and some very strong black coffee sounds like a great way to start the day." He approached the counter and leaned against it. "So, how are you managing?"

"I'm trying to be normal."

"It won't work."

"Huh?" She tilted her head. Damn, she looked good in the morning. Her complexion, devoid of cosmetics was clear and smooth, with a slight blush on her cheeks. The freckles over her nose were cute, and her eyes sparkled. Even with her hair, tied into a severe ponytail looked attractive.

“You never were normal.” He chuckled, trying to lighten the mood.

“Thanks.” She forced a smile.

“I know that it’s been difficult dealing with the uncertainty and fear.”

“You have no idea. This is my inn and I’m responsible for my guests. I had one die under rather unusual circumstances. I’d like to know why this person decided to commit a crime in my inn, with my knife used on my guest? There are plenty of other inns, not that it would have made it less tragic. But, why me?”

“That’s a good question. By coincidence, or on purpose?”

“You think that someone may have targeted me and my inn?”

“I have to think of all reasons.”

“Joy.”

“I do have a request.”

She stared at him. “What?”

“I’d like your guest ledger. I’d like to do some additional background checks. Though I’ve had coffee with everyone registered so far, I’d like to search further. ”

“You think this might be an inside job?”

“I can’t rule anything or anyone out.”

He watched as she reached under the counter and retrieved her leather-bound journal. She placed it on the counter. “If it helps.”

“I’ll pick it up after I have my coffee and tart. I don’t want other guests seeing me with it. It could raise suspicions, if one of them is my suspect.”

“I haven’t been sleeping well these past nights as it is. If one of my guests is a murderer, I won’t be sleeping at all.”

“Just keep your door locked and have your cell on and nearby.”

“Gee, I feel so safe now.” She rolled her eyes.

"Believe me, I don't want to see anything happen to any more guests, and definitely not to you."

After Darrin went to the dining room for his coffee and tart, Katherine sat pondering behind her counter. As she sipped her very black, strong coffee, her mind wandered. She thought it ironic that she could have both an F.B.I agent and a serial killer under her roof. Who said that the life of an innkeeper was dull? She longed for a return to boredom and monotony.

Ever since the murder, she wasn't sleeping well. Every creak, noise or the opening and closing of doors made her jittery. Every time the volunteer fire department's alarm sounded, she jumped up, wondering if there was another murder. She checked the door to her suite several times, before being assured of it being locked, even pushing a chair under the doorknob as added protection. Her windows were locked, curtains drawn, and her cell phone was on and next to her bed. As usual, the glow of a nightlight cast a dim golden glow. She still trembled and her heart raced with a fear of the unknown.

She had locked the room where her guest was murdered, refusing to rent it out to anyone. Ghosts lurked in such places and would bring bad luck, so she thought. Who would want to sleep in a room where a murder had taken place? She wouldn't. It was bad enough that her inn had been tainted by the crime. Her guests were not aware of the morbid and frightful occurrence, or she would surely be put out of business. That was another reason for her skin to erupt into goosebumps.

The thought that a murderer walked into her kitchen made her tense. Her personal safety had been violated, as if raped. How dare someone enter her private space and steal with the intent to do harm. As a result, she placed her knives in a locked drawer. She pondered her pantry and the food stores. What if the criminal had tainted them? She had poured out and replaced milk, cream, and juice for fear of being poisoned. Her mind had become paranoid with possibilities. The kitchen door was now locked when not in use.

This situation was getting a bit too personal, and she eyed every guest with suspicion. Her guests were informed that the front door would be locked promptly at 2 a.m. If they had to enter later, they would have to ring the doorbell. There was no use taking chances. Every evening she worried about what the night would bring. Somewhere, either in her inn or on the Institution grounds lurked a demented killer. She didn't want any more of her guests, Darrin or herself being the next victim.

"Good morning."

Nina's singsong voice startled her from her morbid thoughts. The woman looked a little too perky and effervescent to be staying at the scene of a murder. Katherine had to remind herself that guests were not aware that a crime had taken place. Nina had no reason to be concerned. They just assumed that the poor man suffered a heart attack. Attired in her painted-on yoga togs, her hair piled atop her head, she held her yoga mat. She flashed her shimmering smile.

"Morning," Katherine replied, forcing a grin. "Ready for yoga, I see?"

"Oh, yes. I am being spoilt here with daily classes. Yoga is good for the mind, body, and soul."

"I'll take your word for it."

Nina glanced toward the dining room. "Tea?"

"All brewed. Plus, I have a special treat, a lemon tart."

"I read about them. Thank you." She turned and walked toward the dining room where Darrin had gone.

Darrin's mind would be relieved of the case for a while, Katherine surmised, with Nina's glamorous presence.

Whatever spat they had would probably melt away like the creaminess of the tarts. Katherine sighed.

She picked up the paper and continued to read. One article caught her attention. It was an interview with the Institution's newest benefactor, Agatha Cromwell. Aunt Aggie sure knew how to make a grand entrance. Donating one and a half-million dollars to The Chautauqua Fund was guaranteed to place her in good standing at the Institution. It was one way to smooth the approval process for her inn.

The North Lake Inn was to be the most modern, state-of-the-art accommodation on the grounds. It would fill a neglected need for upscale, contemporary rooms with lake views and five-star service. Those who preferred to travel in style would no longer be relegated to musty, antique-filled rooms in century-old buildings or dormitories. They would reside in luxury suites, with sitting rooms, kitchenettes, bedrooms and baths with all of the amenities. Each climate-controlled suite would also have a private balcony. An infinity-edge pool would overlook the lake and there would be terraced gardens. The inn would fill a need for a clientele that had been neglected due to tradition and fear of change. At least that's what her aunt told the reporter.

Katherine wanted to scream. The Institution was unique because it held on to old-fashioned tradition. Unlike modern lakefront resorts, it was a throwback to simpler times. People came because once you entered the gates, you were transported back in time. There weren't many places in the country where you could do so. If the Aunt Aggies of the world had their way, commercialism would trump tradition and all would be lost. It was bad enough homeowners with more money than taste had erected monstrous contemporary summer homes on North Lake. The addition of a contemporary inn would be one more travesty. Bowing to the modern world was something that raised her ire. How dare her aunt, like other outsiders, come in with their loaded bank accounts and dare to change the atmosphere of the place!

When Darrin emerged from the dining room, he was chuckling with Nina. Apparently, they made up. Katy had been arranging stems of gladiolas in an old Lennox vase. Cut flowers lay on the counter, while she placed others in the vase filled with water. The pink and white flowers emitted a sweet, familiar fragrance. Chautauqua tradition was to place a vase of gladiolas on one's front porch as a welcome sign of hospitality.

"Pretty flowers," Nina commented, as she and Darrin approached.

"Thanks." Katherine met Darrin's gaze.

Nina frowned at the exchange.

"That tart was fabulous," Darrin said. "Didn't you like it, Nina?"

She nodded. "I'd best be off to my class to work it off."

Nina turned abruptly and left, the screen door banging behind.

Darrin shook his head. "She's an unusual woman, charming and moody."

"Must be a bad case of PMS," Katherine mumbled.

Darrin picked up a stem and sniffed it. "Brings back memories."

"Good and bad?"

"You know, being here has caused me to do a great deal of thinking."

"About the case?"

"About you." He once again met her gaze and, this time, a warm flush overcame her, the same effect he had on her in her youth.

"Why would you bother to think about me? I'm just another memory."

He leaned on the counter. "I always wondered why you never answered my letters."

"Letters? What letters?" Her heart skipped a beat.

"The ones I sent after the fire. I kept writing, but the letters were returned unopened."

"I … I never received any letters." A lump formed in her throat.

"I wrote to you and sent them to your aunt's house."

She shook her head. "I never got any letters."

"Weird. Think your aunt intercepted them?"

She covered her mouth. Her aunt! The bitch! She wondered why she hadn't heard from him. He had promised to write and she didn't receive anything and figured that he had just moved on. Her heart had been broken into tiny pieces, thinking that he had forgotten about her, their history, and their dreams for the future.

"It would be just like my aunt." She uncovered her face and drew a deep breath.

"Damn the days before e-mails and texting." He banged the counter with his fist.

"My aunt would have never allowed me near a computer or a cell phone, trust me." Damn, her aunt!

"I wrote to you. When I didn't get an answer, I assumed that you gave up on me, on us."

Her lips trembled. "I wouldn't have given up on you."

"Oh, Katy." He grasped her hand. "You're shaking."

"Imagine, I never knew. Had you not returned here, I never would have known. I thought that because my father caused the fire that ruined your life, I was to never be a part of it. I thought that you hated me because of what happened.

She couldn't hold back the tears that began to drizzle down her cheeks. She choked back more tears.

"Don't cry."

"I can't help it."

He reached over the counter, drew her head into his hands and kissed her on the lips. It was a measured kiss of comfort and concern. Their eyes met. He smiled, saying, "I had to find some way to stop you from crying."

Another voice startled and parted them, "I forgot something."

Nina was standing in the doorway, her face aflame. She raced past them and bounded up the stairs.

CHAPTER 19

"What the hell was *that* about?" Darrin asked, as Nina's footsteps were beard stomping up to the third floor.

"Jealousy?"

"I hardly know the woman." Darrin shook his head. He had only taken her out once and exchanged small talk. Hell, she wasn't Katy.

"I guess she'd like to know you better."

"The only woman I'd like to get to know is you, Katy. I'd like to hear about your life after the fire and your life here."

"It's not as exciting as Nina's, I'm sure." She shrugged.

"Hey, Nina is interesting but she's not you. I don't share a history with her. I've never kissed her."

Gazing into her eyes was like going back in time when they were both young and innocent, before the fire and life had hardened them. Kissing her was like reliving their first kiss. All of the mystery, wonder, and promise reappeared. The longing, the softness of her lips, the heat of her embrace and his body's quick reaction were still there. No one ever had that complete effect on him. He didn't come back to rekindle their romance, but seeing her ignited old feelings, thoughts, and dreams. He wondered if she felt the same.

"Maybe destiny called us back here," he said.

She scoffed. "Are your kidding?"

"Isn't it a little strange that we would both end up here after being separated and living across the country?"

"Nothing surprises me in life anymore."

"When this case is solved and I have more free time, I'd like to get to know you better, Katy."

"I don't see why. I'm rather boring." She reached behind the counter and handed him the leather-bound ledger. "If I recall, you wanted to review this."

He took it, placing it under his arm. "Thanks. I know what I'll be doing most of the day. By the way, you're not boring."

Nina came down the stairs, grasping a tote bag. With a quick glance their way, she headed out the door without a word.

"Maybe you can dig up some dirt on her." Katy's voice had a bite to it.

"No one is immune from this investigation. I'd better get to work."

"Me, too."

As he walked toward the stairs, he turned to see Katy taking the vase of gladiolas out on the front porch. Though life had dealt her difficulties, she was still a wholesome, feminine woman with an air of dignity about her. Shopworn and worldly she was not. He liked that. He liked it a lot.

Seated on the porch outside of his room, he worked on his laptop. He sat back on the cushioned wicker loveseat, the computer perched on his lap. The ledger lay opened on the nearby coffee table. A slight breeze wafted up from the lake, though the skies were blue and sunny. Except for the sounds of birds chirping and distant voices, the atmosphere was blissful. He assumed that most of the guests were at the morning lecture in the amphitheater and the reason why the grounds were quiet. He inhaled a deep breath of fresh air and continued to tap a name with the keys. Nina Marie Wailson.

He had gone through the ledger investigating each guest in depth. Nothing stood out to raise his suspicions. Everyone seemed legal and legitimate, most without so much as a traffic ticket. They had histories with education, professions, and families. They had photographs and homes. None were in the medical or pharmaceutical field.

"I saved the best for last," he muttered under his breath, anxious to see what he would find on the elusive, and temperamental Nina.

Expecting to find some smoking gun, he was disappointed. Though older than she appeared, there wasn't anything to raise his suspicions. She had been born into the British aristocracy. Her father was a Lord and she lived in a large manor house surrounded by manicured grounds and forest. Educated in private schools and at Oxford in language and education, she lived the life of a jetsetter. She traveled the world, living and experiencing different cultures until she tired of them. On a whim, she traveled to the United States and had been traveling between New York City and Los Angeles for the past few years. She appeared to be nothing more than a spoiled little rich girl, rather close to a middle age woman.

He snapped closed the laptop. Rubbing his eyes, he rested his head against the backrest. So far, he had gone over the list of employees, full-time and Seasonal residents, weekly guests, who had arrived so far. He'd researched guests at the inn thoroughly in-depth, and had yet to find anyone suspicious. He was missing something. Someone on the grounds was his suspect, yet she had covered her tracks and watched her back.

He knew that there was no such thing as a perfect crime. Most criminals eventually slipped up and were caught. Serial killers, in particular, seemed to like to play cat and mouse games. They liked to taunt and get caught. This one had upped the ante by increasing the number and frequency of her crimes. She had returned to her hunting grounds and instead of picking her prey, she was killing them. Procuring money, that had seemed to be her primary goal, was no longer her incentive. So far, two innocent men visiting the Institution were dead, and there were six more weeks left in the ever-important Season. He had to stop this criminal before more lives were lost. His supervisor at the NYC office was seeking closure. The report of two new deaths did not bode well for Darrin.

"No pressure," he said aloud. Right.

To clear his head, Darrin decided to go running. Running always provided stress- relief. Instead of the treadmill, he decided that the clear, sunny day was ideal for a jaunt around the grounds. Damn the memories. He'd run near the lake, avoiding the location where The Carter Inn once stood. He didn't know if he could ever visit the place where his parents' inn stood, and where his memories ran deep. He donned shorts, tee shirt and running shoes. In the lobby, he noticed that Katy was away from her counter perch and it made him smile. He hoped that she was actually doing something fun for once.

He started south, taking the red brick walk past the Parthenon-like Hall of Philosophy, the pillared Hall of Christ, clapboard Alumni Hall and cute Chapel of the Good Shepherd. He crossed Thunder Bridge and jogged around the south end to South Lake Road. Following the blacktop road by the lake was scenic and refreshing. He had always loved Chautauqua Lake, with its rippling water, docked sailboats with their towering masts, and the ducks and ducklings paddling about near shore. He passed the Sailing Center, the camps, fitness center and continued on where South Lake merged into North Lake past the Athenaeum, Palestine Park and Miller Park, and up he hill toward the North side where large homes loomed over the lake. At University Park, a woman's voice coming up from behind startled him.

"Great day for a run," she said, catching up and running beside him.

He recognized the trim blonde. Though her hair was pulled back in a tight pony tale, her gray eyes were piercing and memorable. Her tank top hugged her curves like cling wrap, her shorts barely covering her tight ass.

"Remember me? Agatha Cromwell." She spoke clearly as if she hadn't broken a sweat.

"Oh, yes," he replied, swiping at perspiration that drizzled down his face and dampened his tee shirt.

"See that lot over there?" She pointed to a vacant grassy lot. "That's mine."

"Your future inn?" He stopped running and stretched.

"The most modern on the grounds." She stopped to face the lot.

He looked at the overgrown lakefront lot. "Remember, modern is a bad word around here."

"Mr. Wentworth, bite your tongue."

Oh, yes, he was Brantley Wentworth.

"Sounds like you have big plans."

"Construction is to begin after the Season. Heaven forbid should there be any construction or noise during the famous Season." She laughed in a haughty way he found a bit annoying.

"I'd better be heading back," he said turning south.

"Are you still staying at that dreadful Honeysuckle Inn?"

"I actually like it. Maybe I'm a glutton for punishment."

"There are fun forms of punishment," she mumbled.

"Hey, I'll race you to Bestor Plaza." He figured that a real race would be the punishment she deserved, especially having to run up the steep hills.

"You're on."

He gave her a head start. She took off like a thoroughbred out of the gate. It seemed that no matter where he went on the grounds, he encountered overly social women. Agatha Cromwell was another one worth investigating a bit more closely.

He let her reach Bestor Plaza first.

"I won!" She pumped her fist in the air, gasping for breath.

He smiled at her Rocky imitation.

"What do you say we grab a bite at Afterwords?" Catching her breath, she pointed to the stairs leading up the Afterwords Café that was located above the bookstore, next to the post office.

"He pulled at his damp, clinging shirt. "I'm not fit to be seated next to anyone. I'd clear the restaurant."

She sized him up with raised eyebrows, and bit her bottom lip.

He glanced over at the steps leading from the post office and met Katy's icy gaze. She tilted her head as she looked from him to Agatha. She was holding a stack of letters and a package that she looked like she might drop.

"Hi Katy," he greeted with a smile.

She stopped at the bottom of the stairs. "Hi."

Katy's manner was serious and peeved.

"So if it isn't my beloved niece," Agatha said, hands on her slim hips.

Niece? Darrin froze in his tracks. Katy had a reason to be upset. No wonder this woman knew so much about Katy and the Inn, and was so filled with animosity.

"Aunt Agatha, I didn't know you and Mr. Wentworth met." There was a bite in her voice.

Aunt Agatha? This aging femme fatale was the wicked aunt Katy told him about? The witch who withheld his letters, and treated Katy like a servant?

"Yes, dear, we had dinner together at the Athenaeum the other night and met while running today. I showed him the location of my inn." Agatha's capped smile sparkled.

"I see. I hope that you both have a wonderful afternoon together as well." Katy turned on her heels and walked away.

Darrin could see the pain on her face and the hurt in the crack in her voice. Just when he thought that he was winning her over, another woman interfered. First, it was Nina. Now, Agatha. Agatha was gloating, making her niece believe that something was going on between them to somehow harm her. He knew that her aunt had no way to suspect that he was Darrin, the boy she had kept away from Katy for so many years, the man who still cared for her. Her aunt wanted to hurt her for the sake of just hurting her. He couldn't understand why.

"I didn't know that my innkeeper was your niece," he said, trying hard not to give away his anger, lest she wonder why he was upset.

She sighed. "Sadly, yes. I don't know how she can stand to live in that house, yet alone run an inn. That place has ghosts, I swear Katherine herself, is haunted."

"I've been there for two weeks." Yeah, right, he hadn't seen any ghosts, just a murder.

"Better watch out for things that go bump in the night." She winked.

"I will. I'll take a rain check." Right, when hell froze over. He couldn't wait to get away from the woman.

"By the way, avoid the master suite on the second floor. It's especially haunted, since a suicide took place there." She chuckled before jogging away.

The second floor suite? Wasn't it the location of the bathroom where Katy's mother slit her wrists? Wait … Wasn't that *his* suite?

CHAPTER 20

Katherine practically ran back to her inn. Tossing the mail on the counter she walked around it and perched on her stool. Being seated didn't stop her knees from knocking and her body from shaking. Her heart raced from the fast walking and from the stress of seeing her aunt with Darrin. Not only was she standing beside him, she was flirting. They both were glistening after a long run about the grounds, she surmised.

Darrin's investigation was getting a bit too intimate.

She had escaped her aunt by returning to Chautauqua, the last place she thought Agatha would want a part of. The ghosts of the past were returning to haunt her, all of them: Darrin, Agatha, and death. This wasn't fair. Hadn't she suffered enough?

A letter on top of the mail pile caught her attention. It was handwritten in fine script and the postmark was from California. The name on the address label was Troy Adams, an unfamiliar name. The letter instilled another sense of foreboding and it didn't make sense. She had often received correspondence from out-of-towners seeking accommodations for the Season, the winter ski season, or the next year. Something about this letter told her that it was unusual and unexpected. She gingerly picked it up, as if weighing it. Pondering, she read the name and address several times. Taking a deep breath, she grabbed a brass letter opener and slit it open. With trembling fingers she withdrew the fine linen letter. Unfolding it, she saw that it was neatly handwritten in legible script. It resembled a personal letter and not business.

She read in silence.

The words, perfectly formed and succinct held a message that was both shocking and frightening. If seeing Darrin and Aunt Agatha was enough to frighten her, the contents of this correspondence were enough.

"Oh my God!" she shrieked out loud. Never in a million years had she expected a letter to turn her life upside down, and inside out.

At that moment, the screen door to the inn burst open and Darrin was in the lobby before her, pistol drawn.

At the sight of him holding the gun, she screamed.

They stared at each other with wide-eyes surprise.

"What … what are you doing?" she yelled, wondering why he held a gun.

"You screamed. I thought that you were in trouble." He slid the pistol into the leather holster he had around his waist, under his baggy cargo shorts. Ever since the last murder, he had taken to wearing it regularly, along with a set of cuffs.

"And you were going to shoot me?" The letter in her hand was waving like a flag.

He shook his head. "Hell, no. I thought that someone was hurting you."

"I'm all alone."

"That's a good thing. Why did you scream in such a panic?"

"I … I received some startling news." She waved the letter.

"Must be some really bad news." He faced her.

"I don't know. It's shocking." Tears started to form in the corner of her eyes and drizzle down her cheeks.

"Okay, you don't have to share it with me."

"Why would I share it with you, if you are now hanging out with the wicked witch of the east."

"Who?' He scrunched his eyebrows.

"Aunt Aggie."

"That woman? She's a piece of work, definitely a suspect. You think that I'd have anything to do with her if I weren't on this case?"

"I don't know what to think any more."

"What's with the letter?" He pointed to it in her shaking hand. "Is it worse than your aunt?"

"I don't know."

"Okay, you don't have to share." He turned around to leave.

"Wait."

He turned to face her.

"If I have to deal with one more thing alone, I'll die."

He went behind the counter and reached for her arm, drawing her out from behind. She resisted, not wanting to leave her post.

"Katy, you have to stop using that counter as your security blanket. Can't you see that it's nothing more than a self-imposed prison? It's keeping you from the freedom you deserve and need to experience."

"Don't…" More tears rolled down her cheeks that she couldn't control. He was reaching into her psyche. Sitting behind the counter was her comfort zone, the place where she could be in control and secure. Away from it, she was vulnerable and afraid. With recent incidents, she sought more security. She couldn't admit it, even to herself.

He touched her arm. "Let's go sit in the parlor and discuss the letter."

She drew a deep breath for courage and allowed him lead her away from the counter, toward the parlor. On unsteady legs, she entered the parlor and sat on the velvet-upholstered settee. He sat next to her.

"Even you have to admit, this is more comfortable."

She nodded, sniffling.

He withdrew a linen kerchief from his pants' pocket and dabbed at her tears. He gave it to her and she dabbed the corner of her eyes.

"The letter?" he asked softly.

She handed it to him. "You read it. I can't explain."

He took he paper and began to read.

She noticed the expressions change on his face from solemn lines to a grimace as he read each line, shock registering at the end.

"Oh, my," he said with a deep sigh.

"Can you believe it? Should I believe it? Is this some kind of sick joke?"

"It seems real. I can conduct a little background research, if it would make you feel better."

She nodded.

"For now, let's assume it's real."

"So, I am to believe that while married to my father David Morrow, my mother had an affair with this Troy Adams?" Her heart was racing. Her devoutly religious and conservative mother had an affair?

"Sure sounds like it. He says that he suspects that you are his biological daughter, and he wants a DNA test to prove it."

"It's taken him this long to figure it out?"

"He claims that David Morrow was biologically incapable of fathering children."

"And why I don't have siblings?" Her life was unraveling in a way so mysterious it was difficult to comprehend.

"Apparently."

"And he's coming out here to visit me?"

"Sounds like the plan."

"Oh my God. First Aunt Aggie, and now this man?"

"Hey, on a more positive note, if this man is your real father, Aunt Aggie isn't your biological aunt." He grinned, placing his arm around her shoulders that she found comforting.

She smiled at the thought.

"See, there's some positive news in this."

"You think? So far, the events and news around here have been rather grim."

Just when she thought she had reconciled with the past and moved on, her history had come back in full force, like a tornado uprooting her life. She worried about surviving the onslaught and rebuilding her life after this storm.

CHAPTER 21

Ever since Agatha's revelation about his suite, Darrin was uncomfortable. He had quizzed Katy, and she admitted that it was once her parents,' but that it had been completely renovated and updated. She never alluded to her mother's suicide having taken place in it. He assured himself that the bathroom was completely new, and all vestiges of the past were history. Ghosts did not exist, he assured himself and if they did, her mother's ghost had no reason to haunt him.

The case, however, was haunting him. First, he was at the Institution with its memories. Second, he was reunited with his past through Katy. Third, he was staying in her parents' home and suite. Fourth, the theme of his visit was death. From the tragedy of the past, to his assigned case and victims to the murder that took place down the hall, death engulfed him. The fear of more deaths gnawed at him as well.

The fourth week of the Season was beginning and Darrin was concerned. Would the mysterious murderer strike again? He had to make progress in the investigation before another life was lost. He seemed no closer to the suspect than he had when he first arrived. This woman was calculating and shrewd.

He had researched the names on his list thoroughly and, with the beginning of a new week and a new day, had more names to pursue. He doubted if they would offer any clues, since two deaths occurred prior to their arrival. Someone who was on the grounds long-term offered his best hope, yet none of the names he investigated raised any red flags.

Katy's Aunt Agatha could have made a great suspect but she had such a public profile that it seemed unlikely. She had several husbands, but all but one of the marriages ended in divorce. Her real name was on all of the marriage certificates. Though she was a gold digger, her personal fortune made it unnecessary. She also had a stake in the Institution, and he couldn't see her tarnishing its stellar reputation when she had too much too gain from it.

With serial killers, you never knew. People who seemed so successful and so together were not exempt from committing heinous crimes. Motives were as varied as those committing the crime. He couldn't rule anyone out.

The best he could do was keep an eye out, and hope that the killer would make a mistake. Lapses in judgement and big mouths often flushed them out.

He leaned back in his bed, snapped shut his laptop and rubbed his eyes. It was getting late. Darkness and an eerie stillness descended over the grounds. There was something about the night that bothered him. Ever since the fire at his parents' inn, he found the evening unsettling. Instead of sleeping, he often found himself alert. He was like a night watchman standing guard until daybreak, when light would overcome the darkness and the world outside would once again be visible and safe. Irrational? Yes. He had learned to exist on little sleep and short naps during the day.

"Damn it, I'm a vampire," he whispered with smirk. The only blood he was after, though, was a killer who preyed on old men.

With the thought of old men came a replay of his conversation with Katy earlier in the day. A man claiming to be her real father had written her a letter, and was planning a visit to see her.

What a strange turn of events. As if Katy wasn't dealing with enough stress: his return, the poisoning, the murder at her inn, and her greedy aunt. Now, she had an absentee father.

He closed his eyes trying to remember Katy's parents. Her father was debonair, the epitome of tall, dark, and handsome. He was fashionably preppy, with a snobbish sophistication. As a boy, Darrin thought that he looked down on him as an inferior. David Morrow had been educated in New England boarding schools and at Yale. He was a successful financier who seemed to have it all, and yet never had enough. Katy's mother was a trophy on his arm. Ten years younger, she was petite, thin with delicate features, golden hair, and a quiet demeanor. She acquiesced to her husband, who treated her like a child more than a wife. Whereas, he was the center of attention, she blended into the background.

Katy was doted upon by her kindly mother, and criticized by her domineering father. Nothing she could ever say or accomplish was ever good enough for him. He never let her forget that he wanted a son. She would be his only child and he often ignored her. Perhaps, knowing that she wasn't his biological child was reason for his discontent.

Darrin recalled how Katy would fall into his arms quaking in tears over her father's neglect, and lack of affection and concern. The more she tried to gain his favor and concern, the more he abandoned her physically and emotionally, the same treatment he had afforded her mother.

It was sad to witness because Darrin's parents were quite the opposite. He was a treasured only child, and treated like a gift. His parents hugged and kissed him, told him he was loved, encouraged, and supported him. He was the center of their universe.

The fire ended it. However, his aunt and uncle adopted him and treated him as one of their own. He was never wanting for love, attention, and encouragement. After being reunited with Katy, he realized that fate had not been as kind to her. Her aunt Agatha had been as cold and self-centered as her father. Iced blood must run in some families.

He sighed. Katy deserved more. She had ambition and determination but something was holding her back. Her low self-esteem had turned into fear. He had to get her to experience life, instead of having it revolve around her.

His cell phone rang. *Please let it be a lead and not another murder.* He eagerly answered it, "Hello?"

"I hope I'm not disturbing you?"

"Katy? Is something wrong?" It was the first time she dialed him and there was a tremble in her voice.

"Yes and no."

"Huh?"

"Troy Adams' flight is landing at Buffalo-Niagara International Airport at 8 a.m. in the morning. He'll be grabbing the shuttle to get here."

"Okay. That's a good one and half-hour ride."

"I was wondering if you could wait with me."

He hesitated. It was an odd request.

"I … I'm sure I can."

"I don't want to inconvenience you, but I don't want to face him alone."

Now he understood her trepidation. The man may be her biological father, but was still a stranger. To answer any doubts he had conducted a background check on the man. He was an upstanding citizen, a successful retired executive.

"Well?"

"Only for you, Katy. Only for you."

By 9:00 a.m., Darrin was showered, dressed, and downstairs. He caught Katy removing a tray of steaming

cinnamon rolls from the oven as he ambled into her kitchen. He liked the way she leaned over, her blouse open enough to show the curve her breasts, her firm behind, and had the urge to touch her. Knowing better, he just smiled at the thought, ignoring his body's frisky reaction. He drew a whiff of the spicy sweet scent and his stomach rumbled.

She placed the tray on the stainless counter to cool before transferring the buns to an antique china serving platter. After, she met his gaze and he could sense the trepidation in her eyes. She reached back to untie the frilly apron about her waist.

Darrin moved to help, his hands brushing hers as he undid the bow and knot and helped ease the white linen off. He set it on a nearby chair.

"Thanks." She tucked her plaid blouse into her waistband and smoothed her khaki slacks.

"You look fine." He sensed her unease.

"You think?"

"I know."

She smiled. "I have fresh coffee brewing, hot water for tea, and a pitcher of orange juice. The guests already had their breakfast. This batch is for us."

"Your dad will be impressed."

She tilted her head. "You mean, Mr. Adams?"

"Yes." She wasn't accepting it as fact. Without the DNA test, it was conjecture.

She handed him the platter of rolls. "Take these into the sunroom, and I'll get the beverages. What time is it?"

He glanced at her wall clock, "About 9:30."

She drew a deep breath and sighed. He could understand her jumbled nerves. It wasn't every day when your family tree suddenly changed. Her life had undergone many changes but this could be a big one.

He carried the tray into the brightly lit conservatory and set it atop a wicker table. Sun streamed through the glass walls, adding a comforting warmth. It was a positive setting for a reunion.

Katy came in with a silver tray laden with a coffee and teapot, creamer and sugar bowl. "I think we're all set."

Like clockwork, the screen door to the inn opened. Katy spun around to face the lobby, her hands fisted at her side. Darrin stood next to her.

"Deep breath," he said.

She drew a deep breath, closing her eyes for a moment.

"Hello," a man's deep voice bellowed from the foyer.

"Please come in. We're in the conservatory," she invited, lips quivering in a smile.

Footsteps squeaked on the plank floor.

A tall man, dressed formally in a brown suit marched into the room. A shock of white hair framed his face, that was heart-shaped like Katy's with the same sparkling emerald and amber eyes. He hesitated, staring at Katy. She met his gaze, frozen in place.

Darrin observed the meeting with interest. In his mind, there was no doubt that they were father and daughter. The resemblance was uncanny.

"Katherine?" the man asked.

She nodded and grabbed Darrin's arm as if for security. He could feel her trembling.

"I'm Troy Adams. One look at you, and I am assured that you are indeed my daughter. You are the spitting image of my mother." He shook his head and came closer.

Katy took a step back.

"Is this your husband?" Adams asked, pointing at Darrin.

"I am just a guest and friend, Brantley Wentworth," Darrin introduced, not wanting to blow his cover. He reached out a hand and the man shook it with a firm grip. He could tell that Mr. Adams wasn't convinced of the "just a guest" part.

"One thing about the Institution, it doesn't change but the people do." Adams glanced about the room. "This house changed as well. When did it become an inn?"

Darrin was impressed. The man was more observant than he.

"When I inherited it," Katy said. "It's all that I had … have."

"Beautiful Victorian lady." He sighed, and appeared lost in some memory. "I haven't been here for years … since your mother …"

Katy opened her mouth to speak.

" … stayed with that bastard David Morrow." There was a bite in his voice.

"Um, why don't you come in, sit down and have some cinnamon rolls and a beverage. We can chat," Katy's voice was quivering. She walked away from Darrin, went to the table and picked up a china cup. "May I pour you some coffee?"

Darrin could hear the cup rattling on the saucer.

"Strong and dark?"

"That's the way I like it, too," she said.

He chuckled. "Your father's daughter."

Katy poured the coffee and set it on the table. Motioning to a chair, Adams sat.

Darrin took a cup of coffee Katy offered him and sat across from the sixty-something man.

After pouring her own cup, Katy sat between Darrin and Adams.

"It's funny, I thought I'd never see this place again," Adams said. "Never expected nor planned to. Funny, how when your life is cut short you do all kinds of things you never would have done had you been guaranteed a longer lifespan."

He was a bit pensive.

"Excuse me?" Katy asked, staring at him.

Adams took a sip of his coffee and met her concerned gaze. “I had to meet you before I died. You’re all I have left.”

Darrin swallowed hard, letting Adams and Katy converse while he listened and added support.

“You … you’re dying?” Katherine asked. A sadness and sense of loss overcame her, and yet she didn’t know this man.

He nodded. “I had surgery for pancreatic cancer. I have, maybe several months, maybe several years. Who knows? While I’m still feeling okay and am still mobile I thought I’d fly out to meet you. Just completing unfinished business.”

“I … I’m so sorry about your prognosis.”

“I am, too.” He chuckled, though his eyes held a dark ache. “Oh well, you deal the deck your dealt.”

“How did you know to find me here?”

“Katherine, thanks to the Internet, I tracked you down. I wanted to know what you looked like as an adult, and know what kind of woman you’ve become. Last time I saw you, you were a wee one in diapers.”

“You were there when I was a baby?”

“Yes. I had come back to visit. Do you know how difficult it was hiding in the shadows while another man claimed your flesh and blood? I was David Morrow’s old college friend. I know. What kind of friend could I have been to have fallen in love with another man’s wife, had an affair, and created a baby? I want you to know that I loved your mother. Hell, I wanted her to leave that S.O.B, and marry me to begin a new life in California. For some reason, she decided to stay with David and live a lie.”

"I never knew. My mother never mentioned your name or told me anything. How do I know that you are my real father?" This was surreal.

"Girl, look at me. We are of the same flesh and blood, obvious as all hell. Plus, David Morrow was sterile. He couldn't father children. Radiation for cancer when he was a child prevented it." He reached out and took her hand, squeezing it.

"He knew he couldn't have fathered me?" Katherine's eyes grew wide.

He removed his hand and shook his head. "His family thought it was some kind of miracle that he fathered a baby, and the thought made him feel virile and manly."

"He assumed I was his?"

"I think he wanted to, but knew otherwise."

"My mother and he lived a lie?" She swallowed hard, staring at him in total disbelief.

"Yes. Your mother was such a pious and old fashioned girl, no one would have suspected her indiscretion."

"Did my mother love you?"

"She said that she was in love with me and loved David. It was a strange triangle."

"Did David know?"

"I'm sure he did. He wasn't pleased. He and I had quite a row, and I packed up and left. I flew out West to begin a new life."

"So, you left the East Coast for the West?"

"I left here. That's why it's ironic that I would find you here."

"Excuse me?" The affair happened in Chautauqua? Did every major event in her life happen at the Institution?

"David invited me out here to spend a summer, while I was in grad school and out on break, to visit him and his wife here. I was a guest in this house."

She scoffed. "Some guest, sleeping with the host's wife."

"It wasn't sordid. It was love at first sight. The chemistry was strong and we both knew we were soul mates. It was something we couldn't deny. The attraction couldn't be avoided. We kissed and it led to more, much more." He smiled.

What the hell was going on? Her prim and proper mother had an affair with her husband's college friend under the roof of her home? The idea was out of character it seemed preposterous. Her father couldn't procreate, but lived a lie to boost his ego? To lie to her was beyond cruel. This man Troy was most-probably her biological father? Her head was spinning.

"You knew about the fire?"

"I read about it. Such a tragedy. Such a loss."

"Do you know about my mother?" She stared at him to gauge his reaction.

He stared back. "I heard that she caused the fire when she found David with another woman."

"No. That's wrong." She proceeded to tell him of that ill-fated night when she discovered her mother dead, and raced to get her father, only to get caught up in a whirlwind of fire and smoke. She left out the part about Darrin's leading her to safety, and of his parents. After all, he was Brantley at the moment.

Tears glistened at the corner of his eyes, getting caught in the crow's feet.

She stood and placed an arm around his quaking shoulders. "It was awful, and a night that I will never forget."

Tears drizzled down her cheeks and she looked over at Darrin, whose eyes were also glistening.

"Girl, you have been through a great deal." He looked up at her.

"I have, but I'm a survivor."

"Who took you in?"

"David's sister, Agatha."

"That piece of work?" He sneered. "Had I known, I would have come for you. I was married at the time and we didn't have children. We would have gladly taken you in and raised you as our own. You would have been wanting for nothing."

She rubbed his shoulders and whispered, "It would have been better than the life I led."

He reached up and took her hand. "Marcia would have loved to have raised a daughter."

"Marcia?"

"My wife. We were married fifteen years when she passed. She knew that I fathered you, and would have loved you as her own."

Katy sobbed. Life was so unfair.

"Well, I'm here with you now. Better late than never." He sighed.

"As I recall, you wanted a DNA test?"

"A mere formality. There is no doubt in my mind that you are my little girl."

"Big girl." She forced a smile and patted him on the back before walking back to her seat. She took a sip of her now-cold coffee.

"Do you have a room for me? I hope you don't mind my imposing. I bought a two-week pass in hopes of getting to know you better. I left my bags in the lobby."

Katherine drew a deep breath. She couldn't turn down Adams and send him to another inn. The only room she had left was the one previously occupied by victim Forrest Anderson. He need not know since that fact was between her and Darrin. The murders and lurking killer that were stricken from her mind with Adams' arrival, had resurfaced.

"I can take your bags up, Mr. Adams," Darrin offered.

"Thank you, young man," Adams said.

When Darrin turned and went into the foyer to retrieve them, Adams turned to Katherine.

"What is your relationship to that nice man?" he asked.

"It's difficult to discuss right now." She smiled and, catching herself, became more serious. "He, he's a guest."

He chuckled. "Okay, I'll accept that explanation … for now."

He reached for a cinnamon roll. "You baked these?"

"Yes, and they're probably as cold as the coffee right now."

"Doesn't matter." He took a bite. "Wonderful."

"So, tell me about your life?" she asked.

"Only after you tell me about yours." He winked. "Over dinner tonight? I see that there are some restaurants around here."

"Sounds like a plan."

She smiled. Having Troy Adams enter her life was like a breath of fresh air in the staleness of her routine. Yet, death even permeated their meeting. He was destined to die of natural causes, and not at the hands of a murderess. Having him in her life, even for a short time, was better than not having him at all. She was determined to make the best of their two weeks together. Perhaps, she would find a missing part of herself in the process.

CHAPTER 22

Darrin had been in Chautauqua for little over a month and was no closer to finding his killer than on the first day. He sat out on his porch with his laptop, as rain pelted the roof above. A cool breeze chilled the air, rustling the wet leaves on the surrounding trees. A mist and low-lying clouds hovered over the choppy lake. He drew a deep breath of misty air as he leaned back in his wicker chair. For someone who thrived on challenges, this case had so far been a lesson in futility.

He was grateful for the dark clouds and all-day rain. The weather was an excuse to avoid the lonely women in pursuit of his company. He wasn't in the mood for small talk and pretending to be the ever-affable Brantley Wentworth III. He glanced at his watch. He had missed the morning lecture, the lunch crowds after, and the lonely ladies in hot pursuit.

His thoughts drifted to Katy and Troy Adams. This morning, when he had gone downstairs for coffee and pastry, he ran into Katy. She was all smiles and danced around the kitchen and inn like a teenager. Her high spirits made him happy. Apparently, the arrival of Adams brought out her good mood.

"Have a nice time with your new dad?" he asked her.

"Wonderful time. " She was beaming. "We had a delightful dinner at the Tally Ho."

"They have a great buffet if you're not counting calories."

"We indulged in the food and in getting to know each other. The sauerbraten was to die for. You know, Troy Adams is quite an interesting man. Actually, he would be a great prototype for your Brantley Wentworth. He founded a very successful computer software company, revolutionizing the tax business."

"You don't say?"

"Yet, he's so humble." She sighed. "My regret is not knowing him sooner."

"Be glad that you've met him at all."

"I know. I just can't help but think how my life would have been different had he and his wife adopted me. His wife couldn't have children. I would have been loved and gone to college."

"You wouldn't be here."

She shook her head. "Probably not. I could have moved on."

"You wouldn't have been reunited with me?"

She stared at him. "If fate meant for us to be reunited, it would have happened somehow," she said before disappearing into her kitchen for more breakfast preparations.

Her words made him ponder as the rain began to pelt him as the wind shifted. He snapped closed his laptop, rose and entered his suite.

Fate. He looked around at the antique furnishings and a chill ran through his body, as thoughts of Katy's mother drifted into his mind. The suite was hers, and where she chose to end her life. How tragic, he thought, that she was married to one man while in love with another. She belonged in California with Troy Adams, yet had chosen to stay behind with their daughter, a choice she surely regretted. Her choices patterned Katy's life and Adams' as well. The decision even impacted his life. If David Morrow were not at the Carter Inn that night, he would have had his parents and the inn.

Fate had him at the Institution pursuing a serial killer. Perhaps it was his destiny to find this person and end the crime spree. In the process, he was able to see Katy. Tragedy had changed their lives and made them different people, with different paths than the ones predestined for them. Out of this tragedy, perhaps they would find their future … together.

He sighed and sat in a brocade-upholstered armchair. Rubbing his temples with his fingers, more thoughts from this morning entered his mind.

After talking to Katy, he had grabbed a cup of coffee and a croissant and went into the conservatory. After sitting at a wicker table, Troy Adams ambled in with his coffee and joined him.

"Morning," Adams greeted, setting down his cup. "Looks like a typical Chautauqua day, chilly with rain on the way."

"Another thing that never changes around here," Darrin replied.

"Yeah, change is a dirty word here." He chuckled. "Hell, I see that the wacky widows still abound."

"What wacky widows?"

"The single old ladies looking for love in all the wrong places." Adams winked.

"Met a few myself. Let's see … Glenda … Mildred…"

"Hey, I met Mildred."

"The Birkenstock with socks lady?" Darrin chuckled.

"One and the same."

"You better watch out."

"Don't worry, I'm on to them." Adams leaned in. " So, I hear that you are also from California and head a software firm. Funny, we've never met. What's your firm's name?"

"Umm, Wentworth Analytics." He shifted in his seat. This man could blow his cover. Thankfully, he was related to Katy and someone he hoped he could trust, if need be.

"Never heard of it. Where are you located?" Adams asked, staring.

Darrin scanned the room. They were alone. Instead of burying himself, he decided it best to come clean. He leaned forward, lowering his voice. "Sir, I have a confession to make. There is no such company."

Adams scooted forward in his chair and pursed his lips into a scowl. "Excuse me?"

"I'm working undercover."

Adams leaned forward as if to hear clearer. "What?"

"Katy knows, and you need to swear to keep it secret."

"I can keep secrets. Go on."

"I'm Special Agent Darrin Carter with the F.B.I. I'm working undercover here to investigate a series of crimes." He hated to share confidences with others but thought it necessary in this case. Adams could blow his cover.

"What kind of crimes?"

"Murder. It's important that no one know for the sake of the Institution, and everyone's safety. I've gone over the line in telling Katy and you. You must keep it top secret."

"You have my silence. Hmmm …"

Before he could utter another word, Nina Wailson bopped into the sunroom. Holding a bowl of fresh fruit and a glass of grapefruit juice, she approached their table.

"May I join you?" she asked. "I really don't want to eat alone."

She flashed her glittering smile. Adams rose and pulled out a chair for her and she sat, setting down her things.

"I'm Nina Wailson," she introduced, reaching out a hand.

Adams shook it, meeting her gaze, "Troy Adams."

"Nice to make your acquaintance."

"Have we met before?" Adams was staring at her.

"Have we?"

Darrin observed the exchange, wondering why Adams looked so confused, and Nina so uncomfortable she was fidgeting.

"You're British?"

"Yes. I guess my accent gives me away."

"I visited the U.K. frequently while establishing a branch office in London. Are you from London?"

"Oh, no, Yorkshire." She took a sip of her juice, her gaze unwavering.

Adams banged the tabletop. "Now I know. Are you related to Lord William Edward Wailson?"

Nina choked on her juice. She covered her mouth, coughing.

Adams reached out and patted her shoulder. "Are you all right?"

She nodded.

"I think I've been coming down with a cold. Wretched weather," she said.

"Must remind you of home?"

"Unfortunately." She rose, picking up her bowl and glass. "I'm really not feeling well. I think it best I retire to my room. If you gentlemen will excuse me."

Both men stood and watched her walk out of the room.

"What was that all about?" Darrin asked, after Nina left.

"I must have hit a nerve." Adams arched an eyebrow.

"Lord Wailson is her father," Darrin said.

"That's it! That's how I know her." Adams became animated. "I'll be damned. She's grown up to be quite a beauty. She seems to have had quite a bit of work done. When younger, she was skinny, very plain and homely. Looks like she even shortened the family nose."

"Plastic surgery?"

"A lot. All over." He winked.

Nina was definitely not plain and homely, Darrin thought.

"I've researched all of the guests, even Nina. Yet, so much about her is a mystery. She's also very emotional and territorial."

Adams laughed. "Oh, my. I guess when you're an only child and heiress to a major fortune you can be. Her father was an interesting character."

"How so?"

Adams leaned back in his chair. "I attended Yale with David Morrow and William Wailson. Such party animals."

The connection made Darrin perk up.

"Wills' wife, Nina's mother, had a riding accident when Nina was a teen. Suffered a spinal cord and head injury, and ended up confined to a wheelchair with twenty-four hour care. Wills became quite the dandy and lady's man. Every time I saw him he had a new blonder and younger woman on his arm."

"Did you see him often?"

"In my business, I traveled in the same upper class social circles as the Royals. Wailson was quite the life of the party."

"Did you ever see Nina?"

Adams nodded. "I saw her on occasion. Actually, she took to nursing her mother and seldom left the estate."

"She nursed her mother?"

"With the hired caregivers. She would help tend to her mother's personal needs and learned a great deal about medications and nursing. I thought surely she'd go to school to become a nurse."

The hairs began to stand up on Darrin's neck. Far-fetched thoughts entered his mind. "Did she help administer medications? Give injections?"

Adams chuckled. "Hell if I know. I wasn't there. Young man, I think I know where this is leading."

"Do you?"

"This conversation is beginning to sound like an F.B.I. interrogation."

"This is just interesting, that's all."

Adams leaned forward. "I believe there's a great deal you aren't telling me about your case, but that's okay. If I can help, so be it."

"Was Nina close to her father?"

"Didn't seem to be. It seemed she blamed him for her mother's being an invalid."

"How so?" Darrin was intrigued. "What actually happened to her mother?"

"The way I heard it, from those outside the family, she and Wills had gone riding, had an argument during which her horse reared and she was thrown. No one thought she'd survive, but she did, barely, if you consider living with a brain and a body that don't function."

"Quite tragic."

"Yes, indeed."

"What happened to the mother?"

"She succumbed to complications from the accident about five years ago. Hell, twenty years was a long time to live as a shell of a human, while your husband philandered all over the country." Adams picked up his coffee and sipped. "Damn, this is ice cold."

"I'm sure Katy has more hot coffee."

He shook his head. "I really don't need all of that caffeine anyway. What I could use is a long walk now before it rains." He looked out the window. "Walking seems to be the best way to tour the grounds."

"And the healthiest."

"Whatever that would do with my prognosis." Adams stood and stretched.

Darrin had hoped that Adams would get another cup of coffee and continue the conversation.

"Before you go, what happened to Lord Wailson?"

"Oh, he died shortly after his wife. I heard it was a heart attack. It was shocking because the man was physically fit, and seemed to be in perfect health. He was a health nut, except for his vices of strong brandy and fast women."

Darrin laughed. "I hear that the latter two could do a man in."

"Oh well, Nina was the beneficiary. She inherited everything and could do as she damn well pleased, as I'm sure she has." Adams turned to leave.

"And somehow she ended up here."

"Strange in itself," Adams said, glancing back. "I always thought that there was something unusual about that girl. Very weird."

Darrin had gone over their conversation numerous times in his head. The rain had begun again, pelting the windows and adding dreariness to his thoughts. Was Nina Wailson capable of murder, not once but several times? What motive would she have had when she had inherited more than enough money to live a comfortable life? Why would she risk prison when she had so much freedom?

The thought that the flamboyant and beautiful woman could be a black widow serial killer seemed preposterous. From the descriptions of the murderess from family members of the victims, Nina did not seem to fit. No one described the new wife as being glamorous like a fashion model, unless she had cosmetic surgery after murdering the earlier victims. There was no mention of a British accent but a good actress could mimic any accent or lack of one. A woman with Nina's status, looks, education, and money could attract any man she pleased without preying on lonely old men, unless she had a personal motive. Darrin's mind was reeling.

She had a connection to David Morrow through her father. Recognizing Troy Adams made for a hasty retreat. Were there more connections?

She didn't fit the mold of a killer. Serial killers often didn't fit a mold. All of the behavioral profiling in the world did not fit one particular type of person. Motive was everything.

If Nina were a suspect, what was her motive?

Though it was a long shot, he decided that Nina warranted further investigation. What other lead did he have?

CHAPTER 23

Katherine forgot how good it was to have a reason to smile. Having Troy Adams under her roof was like a breath of fresh air. She wanted to cherish every moment with him. He was her real father. Darrin had the proof. As a surprise, he had fast tracked their DNA tests and surprised them with the results. There was relief in knowing that David Morrow was not her biological father. Now she could call him a bastard without feeling guilt.

The only sadness was the knowledge that her mother could have changed their lives if she had run off to California with Troy. What possessed her to remain married to David Morrow? Who did she really love? She shook her head. Only her mother could answer that question, and she was gone.

While her mind was focused on love, Darrin came down the stairs and into her lobby. He also looked in good spirits, with the hop in his stride and the dimpled grin on his face.

"Good morning," he greeted in an upbeat tone, standing in front of her counter.

"Must be. You look pretty happy for it being so early." It was 6 a.m. He also looked too good in his khaki shorts and form-fitting navy polo shirt.

"Things are looking up," he said.

"The case?" She met his gaze.

"Maybe." He winked.

Interesting, if he had a break with some leads. She thought better of asking and appearing nosy.

"I have an idea. Why don't you join me for a walk on the grounds? The sun is finally out and it's warming up. The inn could survive without you for a bit."

"I, I don't know." She fumbled mindlessly with some papers.

"You do know. You can join me. The question is if you leave your security blanket."

"My what?"

"Put up the out sign and let's go."

"The guests may need something."

"Hey, I saw all the coffee, tea and goodies that you put out this morning. No one is going to starve."

"You really think you have all the answers?"

"Maybe I do." He chuckled, waving his arms toward the door.

Going against her better judgement, she reached down and placed her out/emergency sign up on the counter. Stepping around, she smoothed invisible wrinkles from her jeans before meeting him face-to-face.

"Good girl." He took her by the arm and led her out of the inn and into the warmth of the sun. The sky had cleared to an aqua blue with cottony clouds hovering overhead. The rain of the previous day and night was drying, a vapor lifting off the pavement.

She drew a deep breath for inner strength, inhaling the fragrance of blooming hydrangea. Hummingbirds were fluttering around pots of red fuchsia. Even she had to admit that it was too beautiful a day, during a short summer Season to spend it indoors.

Darrin led the way down to Miller Park, the site of the first Chautauqua Assembly. He stopped at Palestine Park, a miniature scale model of the Holy Land, complete with Mounts Hermon and Lebanon, with Chautauqua Lake representing the Mediterranean Sea. The park was designed in 1895 as a way to instruct teachers and children interested in Bible history.

"Remember how we used to play here as children?" Darrin asked, looking over the peeks and valleys of the grassy park with its small plaster models anchored in cement depicting ancient towns.

Katherine smiled, remembering how he used to hold her hand to prevent her from tripping on the uneven terrain, and how one teacher used to frown upon the practice.

To her surprise, Darrin took her hand in his and proceeded to draw her toward the Bell Tower and the Pier Building, just like old times. He remembered, and his touch was comforting.

He pointed toward the Children's Beach. "Our park bench is still there."

"Of course, you'd remember *that.*" In the evening, it had been their preferred make-out spot as teens. Under the dim lamplight, with moored sailboats and waves lapping the shore, they would be entwined in young love.

Being with Darrin was like going back in time and reliving their history, the positive side.

"Shall we trek north?" he asked.

"Sure. Why not?"

They walked up North Lake Drive watching motorboats skim over the glimmering lake. She abruptly stopped when she saw a construction sign advertising her aunt's new hotel. Construction was set to begin after the Season.

"Oops, forgot about that," Darin said, pulling her away and up the asphalt hill.

Being reminded of Aunt Agatha made her anxiety about being away return, and she began to tremble. She breathed in the misty lake air, trying to quell her nerves.

"You all right?" Darin asked, stopping to face her.

"I'll be okay. Thinking about that woman just makes me sick."

Then, it dawned on her. Aunt Agatha wasn't her real aunt. She wasn't family but only a wicked foster mother, soon to be a memory. Her mood lightened.

She let him lead her on, stopping in front of the President's House, across from University Beach. The grand yellow Victorian with sprawling porch and attached matching gazebo was surrounded by a lush lawn and an assortment of pastel hydrangeas. The home served as both a residence and social hall for the President of the Institution, and where he frequently hosted visiting dignitaries.

"Must be nice," she said, observing the sprawling well-manicured grounds.

"Too much responsibility," Darrin replied.

"I know all about responsibility."

They walked passed other historic homes and more modern mansions perched on the lakefront, with built-in swimming pools and private boat docks. With their ultra contemporary architecture, they seemed more suited to an upscale housing development than a National Historic District.

Stopping at the wrought iron gates of the historic Packard mansion, they peered in at the stately red brick mansion with its carriage house, circular brick drive and sprawling grounds. Built by the founder of Packard Electric in 1917, it was one of the most famous historic structures on the grounds.

"Hey," a man's voice shouted.

They turned. Katherine was shocked to find her father strolling with Aunt Agatha. Didn't he know who she was? Apparently, not yet.

Troy Adams walked toward them with Agatha in tow. Agatha was attired in turquoise skin-tight leggings and sports bra, with a phony smile pasted on her made-up face framed by her fluffy hair. Troy looked deceivingly robust in his cargo shorts and tee. Katherine was not amused.

"I just met this lovely lady while taking a walk," Adams said, casting a smile at Aggie.

"I hate to burst your bubble but that lady is my aunt, Agatha Morrow Cromwell. At least she used to be my aunt," Katherine said, trying to be calm though her stomach was churning.

"Yes, I'm her aunt," Aggie replied in a light tone.

Adams stepped away from her, sizing her up. "You're David Morrow's sister?"

"Why, yes. Did you know him?" Agatha was animated, oozing with her fake charm.

"Actually, I did." Adams' demeanor had become serious and steadfast. "He was quite the bastard, and I heard that it ran in the family."

Katherine swallowed hard. This was getting ugly.

"Excuse me?" Aggie placed her hands on her hips and stood tall.

"I knew him all too well. I'm Troy Adams, Katherine's *real* father."

"What?" Aggie screeched.

"I know that you were privy to the family secret. That's why you treated Katherine like a chambermaid when you took her in after he died."

"So, you're the other man?"

"The only man. David never grew up."

"How dare you!" Aggie was seething. Katherine half-expected smoke to rise from her head.

"I don't know why Julia stayed with him."

"Because he had money and you had nothing." Agatha spit out the words.

"She had me."

"Yeah, a struggling student." She scoffed. "Women like Julia didn't know how to struggle."

Adams closed his eyes and fisted his hands. "I now have more money than David Morrow ever inherited."

"Oh, well, too late. Your loss." Aggie shrugged, turning away. "I'll let you all sort out your problems, I have a run to get in."

She jogged off as if all was right in the world. In her world, it probably was.

"Shit." Adams pumped his fist.

Katherine slung an arm around him. "Everything is going to be okay. We have each other now."

"We do, don't we?" Adams forced a smile. He removed her arm and placed it near Darrin's. "Why don't you and this young man continue your stroll? I'm feeling a bit tired and am going back to the inn to take a nap."

"I really should be getting back to the inn as well." Katherine was thinking about the front desk being unattended. The encounter with Aggie made her a touch vulnerable and uneasy.

"The inn will be there when you're dead and gone. You go and enjoy the weather," Adams urged. "I'll check on things before I go to my room."

"I …"

"Continue our walk?" Darrin asked, before she could respond. He took her hand as Troy Adams walked down the road in the opposite direction.

"I feel like I'm living a soap opera." She shook her head.

"Where do you think the writers get their ideas for soap operas?" He chuckled, lightening the mood.

They walked up Prospect to where it became Palestine, passing the Arts and Crafts Quadrangle, Carnahan-Jackson Dance Studios, Bellinger Hall, Lincoln Dormitory, and Sherwood Studio.

"If I recall, you wanted to be a ballerina?" Darrin jogged her memory.

"I did but Aggie wouldn't pay for my lessons. She sent her no-talent daughters to class instead." It was just another bad memory of a wasted childhood.

"I'm sorry to hear that."

She just shrugged. The past was the past.

They strolled in silence past Lenna Hall, McNight Hall, and the Practice Village rehearsal shacks. The little one room acoustic buildings housed Steinway pianos or space for private music practice.

"You still play?" he asked

"I haven't touched a keyboard in years." Just as she hadn't spoken a word of French. More regret.

They walked in silence.

As they walked up Root, Darrin broke the quiet. "Penny for your thoughts? I'm sure you have many."

"I can't stop thinking about what Aggie said about my mother. Could she really have chosen money over love?"

"I'm sure she wouldn't have been the first, nor would she be the last. There's something to be said for stability and security."

"Even if the future showed promise?"

"But promises don't pay the bills, put a roof over your head, and protect your child."

She sighed. "You've always been practical, Darrin." He also had a great deal of common sense, even as a youth.

"Blame my parents."

They stopped for a moment in front of Norton Memorial Hall, home of the Chautauqua Opera Company. The imposing art deco concrete structure featured *bas relief* sculpture on its façade and an arched, covered veranda.

"Do they still sing all of the operas in English?" Darrin asked.

"Yes, they do. After all it was a request of the Norton family since they did donate the building."

He chuckled. "The only thing that changes around here are the seasons and the people."

Next door was the wood sided Bratten Theater, home of the Chautauqua Theater Company.

"Have you ever attended an opera or a play?" He asked.

She shook her head.

"You really haven't been out much."

"This is the most I've seen of the grounds in years," she admitted. As strange as it was, she preferred to stay at her inn where she was safe from memories. On this day the unease she felt was lifted. Darrin was like a buffer between the Chautauqua of the past, and that of the present.

"That's crazy. Forget the past already, embrace the present, and look forward to the future. It's how I've lived my life."

"Lucky you," she mumbled.

"Katy, we can be held prisoner of the past or break free. I suggest you break out already."

She smiled, knowing that he was right. Like the Institution, she had a difficulty embracing change.

"Hey, why don't we have lunch? Hurlbut Church has great soup, salads, and sandwiches." Darrin pointed out the nearby Methodist Church with its art deco stained glass windows.

"You've really gotten around since you've been here." She thought about all of the lonely old ladies he'd escorted around the grounds since his arrival.

"Shh …" He turned away. "I don't want that cloying Mildred to see me."

"She's still after you?" She observed the woman with her floral socks and Birkenstocks walking in the opposite direction. "The coast is clear."

"These women don't give up."

"Speaking of giving up. Any leads on your case?"

"As a matter of fact, your new dad, of all people, gave me some food for thought. When I get back, I need to conduct some additional research."

"Anyone I know?"

"Maybe." He winked.

"You're not telling me?"

"I think it's best to keep this to myself."

"Okay-dokay."

"You used to say that all the time when we were kids."

"Some things just don't change."

"I'm sure glad we have." He took her hand and led her down the walk by the side of the main stairway and church entrance toward the social hall, where lunch was served.

CHAPTER 24

Nina Wailson. What an enigma. He had suspected her and ruled her out. Here he was suspecting her once again, thanks to Troy Adams' information. He contacted his connections at Scotland Yard for information on Lord Wailson, his wife, and Nina and eagerly awaited their information.

When the e-mail finally arrived within a few days, the attachments were many. The girl most unlikely was looking a bit too suspicious.

Lord Wailson was a philanderer his entire life. Titles and money attracted women and he was a magnet. His wife had to have known of his reputation, but theirs had been an arranged marriage of royal genetics and financial mergers. In public, they appeared well-suited. He was devastatingly handsome, and she a glamorous beauty. In private, theirs seemed to be a marriage of convenience. Each had their extracurricular dalliances. They did produce one child and heiress, Nina. From the reports, Nina was reared by a series of nursemaids and nannies. Her father had been decidedly hands-off and her mother physically doting but emotionally distant.

When Nina's mother was tragically injured in the riding accident, an inquiry had been conducted. Authorities determined that her brain and spinal injuries had been caused by the throw from her horse. The circumstances surrounding the incident were based on Lord Wailson's account, as his wife had been comatose. The accident rendered her speechless and incompetent from the injuries.

Troy Adams stated that an argument had taken place that culminated in the accident. The reports neglected to mention this as fact. Apparently, it was something Lord Wailson had revealed. Further questioning of Troy was in order.

The exposé on Nina was telling but not revealing. As a teen, after her mother's accident, her grades at the posh school she attended dropped dramatically, and her behavior became erratic. She had been suspended numerous times for smoking, drinking, and causing trouble. He surmised that many teens would have acted out after such a tragedy. Yet, she did manage to graduate.

While attending school, and after graduation, she spent a great deal of time at her mother's bedside assisting the paid caregivers. It had been noted that she did take some preliminary nursing classes after graduation. Several pertained to pharmaceuticals. A red flag went off, and Darrin sat back in his seat on his porch.

"She knew a bit about drugs," he mumbled. "Actually, more than a bit."

After rubbing his temples, he went back to his laptop. Maybe he was so desperate for a suspect, that he was reading more into this than needed. Yet, the woman had the medical background to pull off poisoning and lethal injections.

Reading Nina's nursing files, one paragraph stood out. She had been suspended from classes after being accused of stealing pharmaceuticals, Phenobarbital, in particular, from the dispensary. A bit too coincidental, considering that Kenneth Spotzworthy had been injected with the drug before drowning at Heinz Beach.

Reading further, he found that her father used connections to get her admitted to Oxford, where she surprisingly excelled in language and education. Dialects were her specialty. Interesting. Darrin's mind was spinning. Could this talent have been used to disguise her accent and, perhaps, create other accents?

He sighed. All of this seemed preposterous and yet plausible.

The question was, "Why?" Why would a woman who had so much going for her go to such great lengths and great distances to commit murder?

He closed Nina's file and went back to review files on the victims.

Oscar Middleton had married Evelyn, a younger wife, only to die by his own hand after being gas lighted with Risperine. Descriptions of the new, young wife were sketchy at best. She claimed to be a widowed schoolteacher. After receiving a substantial part of the estate, it was discovered that hers had been a stolen identity.

The other victims had, too, been drugged or poisoned. Her identity had been discovered to be false after the funeral and bequeath. Darrin shook his head, wondering how this woman could have acted so fast and gone undetected for so long. Hell, no one took a photograph of her? The men she targeted had children whose concern for their father only appeared after he died, and when a will and money were involved. He shook his head. How very sad.

Thinking about the victims, he perused their photographs. One thing stood out. All of them were the age of Nina's late father. Was it a coincidence or a motive? She certainly wasn't in need of money.

The last victim, Forrest Anderson, had been meticulously and quickly stabbed. His room was only one floor down from Nina's. She had arrived on the scene after the fact, acting surprised yet calm, accepting the public news that he died from a heart attack. Could she be so cold and callous? Could she be as brazen as to commit a crime under her own roof?

He knew that the "Siren" was most likely a typical serial killer: impulsive, irritable, violent/aggressive with a past that included abuse. The motive was to avenge a past wrong.

Was Nina out to kill men who reminded her of her father, to avenge the tragic circumstances of her mother?

Darrin thought that either his imagination was getting out of hand, or that he was on to something. Was that intelligent, beautiful, wealthy and charming woman capable of multiple murders?

His cell phone rang and he answered.

"Darrin, Darrin," Katy was screaming hysterically. "I called 911. It's Troy! I thought he was out and went into his room to clean and he's unconscious on the floor!"

"I'm on it!" He hung up and raced to the room formerly occupied by Mr. Anderson. The Institution's sirens were wailing to summon the rescue squad. He met Katy, who was leaning over her father. Troy Adams was on his side, as if he had fallen on to the wood floor.

"At least he's not dead and he hasn't been stabbed. I checked," she said, voice quivering. Tears were streaming from her eyes.

Darrin knelt beside her and checked Adams' neck for a pulse. Though it was faint, he was alive. He was still and pale but alive.

"I wonder if it was an accident or … or …" Katy was shaking.

Darrin placed an arm around her quaking shoulders. "Help is on the way and we'll find out soon enough. I'll go downstairs to direct EMS when they arrive. Anyone else at the inn now?"

Darrin was thinking about Nina.

Katy shook her head. "No. I had knocked on his door and it was locked, so I decided to come back after cleaning all the other rooms. Since there was no answer, I used my key. That's when I found him."

"You stay here." Darrin rose, left the room and bounded down the stairs to await EMS.

EMS arrived and transported Troy Adams to the clinic in Westfield. After he was admitted to emergency, Troy was stabilized and placed in a draped private room. He was still unconscious when the doctor arrived to speak with them. Darrin held Katy's hand for assurance that things were going to be fine. She still was pale and a bit dazed. The whirlwind of activity had been unsettling, as was the thought that Troy may have been the target of his suspect.

"Mr. Adams is in a diabetic coma. He's suffered from hyperglycemia," the doctor stated, reviewing a chart on his clipboard. "Does he have a history of diabetes?"

Katy hesitated before answering. "He does have terminal pancreatic cancer."

"That may explain the elevated glucose levels in his blood and urine. It can be very serious and life threatening. He arrived here just in time."

"Will he recover?" There was a tremor in her voice.

The doctor smiled. "He'll be fine. We just put in an IV. With some fluids to rehydrate him, he should be good as new. Well, as good as can be with his prognosis."

"When will we be able to speak to him?" Darrin asked. He wanted Troy to explain what happened, if it was indeed related to his cancer.

"I suggest he stay here and rest. Why don't you go and get some coffee. It will be a few hours," the doctor suggested. "And don't worry, he'll be safe here."

Darrin heeded the doctor's advice and took Katy out for coffee. To not have her worry, he exchanged small talk. In the back of his mind, he kept wondering what Adams would have to say. He hoped that the episode was just a result of Adams cancer, yet he had the gnawing suspicion that it could be more involved.

It was late afternoon when Troy Adams regained consciousness. He lay in the bed, draped in a sheet and blanket, an IV drip in his arm and a heart monitor beeping with his vital signs. He smiled when Katy followed Darrin into the room.

"Don't you have an inn to run, young lady?" Adams asked.

"I do but I'm more concerned about you."

Darrin pulled up a chair and had her sit at her father's bedside. He grabbed another chair for himself and sat.

"What the hell happened to you?" Darrin asked. "You gave us quite a scare."

Darrin met Adams' steely gaze and chills ran up his back.

"I don't know if Katherine should hear this," Adams started.

Shit, Darrin thought. This was not a simple diabetic coma from pancreatic cancer.

"Katy is privy to my case. I think we've arrived to the point where she needs to know what's going on."

Katy had a glazed look in her eyes and her lips trembled.

"What … what is going on?" she asked.

"I think I've made a break in the case, thanks to Mr. Adams," Darrin began. "I have a suspect, and if she is involved in this, I am assuming that she's my person of interest."

"The 'Siren?'" Katy gasped.

"Perhaps." Darrin turned to Adams. He reached in his pocket and withdrew a small digital recorder. "I hope you don't mind. I'd like to keep this for reference."

"No problem."

"Let's hear what happened." Darrin drew a deep breath and steeled himself for what he might hear.

"I had just washed up and dressed and was getting ready to go downstairs for some of Katherine's strong coffee and bakery, when a knock rattled my door. I assumed it was the chambermaid and answered it. To my surprise, Nina Wailson stood in the doorway."

"Nina?" Katy gasped, covering her face with her hands.

Darrin draped an arm around her shoulders.

"Yes, Nina. I greeted her and she asked if she might come in."

Adams continued, "I saw no harm in it and let her in, closing the door behind. I assumed that she realized we had met in England and that I knew her father. We chatted for a bit about her father and home. She said that she had to leave and wanted to hug me goodbye, as she no longer had her father and said that I'd resembled him. I wasn't expecting to feel the jab of a needle in my neck, and stumbled backward. She just stood there, sneering and laughed. She laughed. Before leaving, she said, "good night" as I fainted. That's all I remembered until awakening here."

"Let me get the doctor," Darrin rose and rushed from the room.

Darrin flashed his badge and credentials at the doctor and explained the situation. After, he followed him to Troy Adams' bedside. After examining Adams' neck, the doctor had determined that he had indeed been injected with something. Until the revelation, he had no reason to suspect foul play.

"I suspect that Mr. Adams was injected with a glucose solution. Apparently, it wasn't expected that Mr. Adams would be found soon enough to be saved. If he had been on the floor another hour or two, he would surely be dead," the doctor explained.

"I wouldn't have a witness to Nina's murder attempt." Darrin was relieved, though he still had to infiltrate her web. "I think it best that Mr. Adams be admitted to the hospital for his protection under an assumed name. I'd like the records to show that he expired."

"Only for the F.B.I." the doctor said.

"Just temporary, you understand, until I get an arrest."

"So much for a joyful reunion with my daughter, and a vacation," Adams said with a loud sigh.

"You'll have both. Just consider this a minor setback. Katy and I are going back to the inn, and for all purposes will be grieving your sudden demise. I want Nina to believe that she succeeded. No way do I want her to suspect that I have her in my sights. Do you understand, Katy?"

"I ... Yes." She still appeared rattled. Darrin thought it an advantage for having it appear that another guest died under her roof.

"Katherine, you listen to this young man," Adams raised a finger to Darrin. "He cares for you."

CHAPTER 25

For all purposes, another elderly guest in the second floor suite died, a case of bad luck. Troy Adams succumbed to hyperglycemia, and never awakened from his diabetic coma. That was the story Katherine told. She was grateful that most of the guests were weekly, and those witnessing Mr. Anderson's demise were gone. Life would go on at the Honeysuckle Inn.

The most difficult part of living a lie, were her encounters with Nina. Every time she saw the woman with her effervescent smile, glittering eyes, and jaunty bounce in her step, she wanted to scream. She really wanted to reach out and punch her, instead of pretending that she didn't know what was hidden behind that killer body, glamorous looks, and lilting accent.

She still found it hard to believe that the statuesque blonde, who had it all wanted more. Funny, here she was struggling to make ends meet, while Nina was sitting on more money than a person could ever spend in one lifetime. Nina had been educated at Oxford, while she dreamed of college and the education she was denied. The woman could have had any man she desired, and instead killed men, lonely old men. The woman even targeted her father. Nina wasn't aware of Troy Adams being her father. What the hell? Nina jet-setted her way around the world and yet, decided to settle in Chautauqua to commit her heinous crimes. Why? Maybe Darrin had answers but she was befuddled.

Darrin. Ever since Adam's incident, Darrin seemed to make it his purpose to keep a close watch on Nina. She observed him bumping into her at breakfast, running into her in the lobby and being in the right place at the right time to see her on the grounds. Though it was part of his job, she still found his interest in Nina unnerving.

Nina skipped into the lobby as if on cue. A broad smile brightened her face, and her eyes had a glossy far away look. If she didn't know better, Nina looked like a woman in the euphoria of being in love. Right. With Darrin?

"Hi," Nina chirped.

"Hi," Katherine replied, pretending to shuffle papers at her counter. "You look awfully happy today."

"Oh, I am." She giggled. "I had the most marvelous lunch off the grounds."

"Really?"

"At Tasty Acre. You know, that cute little diner not far from the gates?"

"Oh, yes. The food must really be great for you to be so excited."

"The food is wonderful but the company was even better. Did you ever know when you found the one?" Nina asked.

Katherine was so startled, she dropped the papers on the floor. Nina bent to retrieve them and handed them to her.

"Oh, I didn't know I touched a sore spot."

If she only knew.

"I … I actually never found the one," Katherine answered with the truth hurting more than this devious woman need ever know. The thought of Darrin being the one for Nina was making her nauseous.

"Oh." Nina put a finger to her lips. "That's so sad."

"Not really."

"There are many men in the world, many evil men, but when you find the one, you will never let him go. You will do whatever it takes to keep him. Well, I need to get ready to hit the fitness center."

Nina walked away and disappeared upstairs.

Katherine assured herself that Darrin felt nothing for Nina. She was a murder suspect, of all people. It seemed that Nina sure wanted him. A chill ran up her spine to her neck. All of Nina's talk about him being the one was creeping her out. Could Darrin be in danger if this woman suspected that he was not after her romantically?

He's a big boy, she assured herself. He was also in law enforcement. She was worried about him and had to admit that she cared for him a great deal more than she let on. His kiss in the rain still lingered on her lips, as did the kiss at her counter. The way he draped his arm around her just when she needed it, was so comforting and caring. He still gazed at her with the intensity of puppy love when they were together. He never let her forget the past, their past.

Thinking about him made her warm and flush. How dare Nina fall in love with Darrin. She loved Darrin. Loved him? The thought actually entered her mind. She had to admit that she never stopped loving him. He was the one. If something happened to him now, after all those years apart, what would she do?

Katherine sat organizing the papers Nina dropped on the floor. An envelope she hadn't noticed before was mingled among the invoices and brochures. Curious, she slit open the ivory envelope and pulled out a matching note card. Thinking it was an invitation, she sat back to read it.

The words made her shudder.

"Miss Morrow, It would be appreciated if you would leave Mr. Brantley Wentworth III alone. One woman is enough for him and that woman isn't you. If you do not leave him alone, a tragedy far worse than what happened to your mother and father will befall you and your inn. Trust me!"

It was not signed, though she recognized Nina Wailson's swirling script. She shuddered, a cold chill running up her spine. The woman was now threatening her. This was getting too personal.

Darrin strolled in from outside, the wood screen door banging behind.

"Sorry," he said, glancing back at the door and flashing his dimpled smile.

"I really need to do something about that door." She swept her hair away from her face, trying to act as normal as she could under the circumstances.

"Are you okay?" he asked. "You look a bit pale."

"I'm fine." She wasn't fine. She had just been threatened by another woman, because of her relationship with Darrin … Brantley.

"It is heating up outside."

"Really?" She was still cold.

"Are you sure you're all right?" He approached her counter. Noticing the card she still held in her hand, he asked, "More bad news?"

Realizing she still held the card, she debated about showing it to him. "Here, you decide."

He took the card from her hand, meeting her gaze with concern and puzzlement.

She gauged his reaction as he read the script. "Shit."

"How did she know about my parents?" Goosebumps popped up on her arms and she rubbed at them.

"Troy Adams said that he, Nina's father and David Morrow knew each other at Yale," Darrin explained.

"David and Troy knew Nina's father? Did Troy tell her father about David and my mother and the fire at the inn?" It was making sense in a strange and diabolical way that made Katherine shiver more.

"And why she chose Chautauqua?" Darrin stared ahead in deep thought. "I need some answers."

"I heard that you had lunch with the enchantress."

"News travels fast."

"She just went up to her room after chatting." She tilted her head toward the stairs. " I think she's in love with you," Katherine whispered.

"What?" His brows shot up and he stepped back.

'Oh, yes, Women know these things and that cryptic note proves it."

" I figured she just liked me and I was using that to my advantage. Now, I'm really concerned."

"I think you are being prepped for some undercover work," she said, the words slipping out without any thought and she drew her hand up to her mouth.

He laughed. "Oh, my. Don't worry, she's the last woman I'd ever want to be under the covers with."

"Why would I worry? Especially after what we've learned." She removed her hand, straightening to gain her composure as much as she could under the circumstances.

He leaned in. "Because you're the only one I'd want to be with under cover. Note or no note."

She felt the color rise in her cheeks.

Before she could respond, he reached out and drew her face near his. As his lips met hers, her eyes closed automatically to savor his taste and touch.

"Excuse me," a voice shrieked.

Katherine opened her eyes to meet Nina's icy glare and the threat became eerily real.

Nina stood still in shorts, tee shirt, and running shoes. She just stared at them in silence before rushing out the front door, slamming it shut.

"Damn it," Darrin pounded the counter with his fist. "You are so irresistible that I just blew it with my suspect. I just compromised your safety as well."

"I guess you'd better run after her," Katherine said, getting back to reality thinking about his case.

He gave a parting glance and rushed outside.

"I can't wait until his case is solved and over. I want my life back, whatever life I have," Katherine mumbled.

Darrin ran down the steps and down the path leading away from the Honeysuckle Inn. He peered down the street, seeing Nina racing away toward the lake. Following her, he finally reached her side. Thinking he was in good shape, he was winded by the time he reached her. The woman sure could run. Though she glanced back at him, she continued to run away. Finally, he reached out and grabbed her arm.

"Stop," he called.

She resisted. "Why?"

"Because I want you to."

"Go back to the hired help." She tried to pull away.

He reached out with both hands and she came to a halt.

Facing her, he said, "We have to talk."

"What is there to talk about?"

Were those tears rolling down her cheeks? Did the woman actually have feelings and emotion? He let go of her.

"Understand, Nina, we do not have a relationship. We are just friends."

"What is she?" Nina pointed up the road toward the inn.

"Someone I loved long ago."

"And still love?"

"Maybe." He was analyzing her reactions.

She sniffled and regained her composure.

"Have you ever been in love?" he asked.

She froze.

"Have you?" he asked again.

"No," she replied in an icy tone, as cold as her demeanor had become.

"Why the hell not? You have everything going for you."

She shrugged. "Everything? I never had everything. You don't understand. No one understands. No one will ever understand."

"Understand what?"

"My past."

"What about your past?"

"Why should I share anything with you? You don't love me. No one has ever loved me. I can't make anyone love me. Why would they want to love me?"

"Why?"

"I'm damaged goods."

"I don't see why."

"I just am. Let it go at that." She turned away.

"What is the issue, Nina?"

"I don't owe you or anyone an explanation."

"Maybe talking about it will make you feel better."

She scoffed, and turned to face him. "Brantley, I'm not who you think I am."

As if he were really Brantley Wentworth III. He wondered what she'd do if she realized he was really an F.B.I. agent.

"Who are you?" he asked, wondering if she would confess and make his case and his life easier.

"She placed a hand on his chest. "I'm a woman who has suffered greatly her entire life, who has never known love until I met you. You're the first man I have ever fallen in love with."

She buried her head in his chest. He placed his arms around her to offer comfort yet from the bite in her voice, there was no doubt that she was troubled. He wanted to believe that she was just a woman yearning for love, yet in the back of his mind wondered if she was capable of murder in her quest to find it.

When she lifted her head and stepped back, she was smiling. Her emotions were like a faucet, running hot and cold.

"I forgive you for kissing her," she said, acting coy and kittenish. "But only if you take me out to dinner tonight, and promise to share a nightcap in my garret."

He pondered for a moment. Having dinner and drinks alone with Nina were not something he had in mind. Now, if it were Katy ...

"Come on, Brantley." She oozed with charm, fluttering her dark lashes and beaming those baby blues.

"Okay," he agreed, swallowing hard. This could be the break in the case that he needed. Maybe getting Nina in a vulnerable position, not in bed, she would let down her guard. He had one witness, Troy Adams but he wanted more, solid proof that she was the "Siren."

CHAPTER 26

"Nina went to the salon to have her hair done, manicure, pedicure ... the works. I'd say she has a hot date," Katy said when Darrin stopped by her front counter after a stint on the computer in his room.

He had spent some time communicating with his field office, explaining his findings to his supervisor. Though Nina was his suspect, they agreed that she needed further investigation. Little did he think that investigating meant agreeing to a date and drinks would be part of the deal.

His investigation began as an undercover operation pretending to lure a black widow by posing as a likely victim. He did meet and socialize with many desperate women in his quest for a suspect. None had appeared to be a likely candidate. Nina seemed the least likely, until Troy Adams arrived. With Adams as a victim and witness, Nina was on the radar. Yet, he needed more proof. Eight men had been murdered, two on the Institution grounds. He would have to tie her to all of the murders to have a solid case, and he needed a motive.

Nina had alluded to her past. She called herself damaged goods and somehow unworthy of love. Her relationship with her father seemed tenuous. There was the mystery surrounding her mother's death. She had a medical background. There was the attempted murder of Adams. She gave Katy a threatening note. All of these were red flags.

In addition to providing details of the evening with his NYC field office, Darrin informed the Chautauqua Police Department and the Chautauqua County Sheriff's Department. If he needed assistance, he wanted other law enforcement to be prepared to act.

He showered, shaved, and dressed for the evening. Thoughts of how to proceed with Nina kept running through his head. The "Siren" was lethal and he had to be prepared to act. He slipped some test strips in his jacket pocket in case she spiked his drink. A cotton turtleneck was part of his attire, to keep his neck covered. He hesitated about carrying his pistol. A firearm offered security but came with risk, should she discover it. He assured himself that he could take care of himself without it. He did stick a pair of lightweight handcuffs deep in his pants' pocket just in case. Early in his career he had gone undercover to nab drug traffickers and, yet, this operation seemed more dangerous.

"Hell hath no fury like a woman scorned," he muttered as he combed his hair in the vanity mirror.

Checking his wristwatch, it was 6:15 p.m. and he was meeting Nina in the lobby at 6:30 p.m. If only he were prepping for a date with Katy. Her face was the one he wanted to see, her eyes the ones he wanted to set his gaze, and her lips the ones he wanted to kiss. When this case was over, he intended to take a break and focus exclusively on Katy. Holding that thought would get him through the evening.

He was grateful that the lobby was quiet when he descended the stairs. The thought of descending into hell was more like it. The out sign was on the counter. The light was dim with only the wall sconces offering a subdued mellow glow. Thank goodness that Katy was away. Seeing her lovely face would have made things even more difficult.

Taking a deep breath, he stepped toward the door and looked out the screen as shadows were overtaking the sun.

"Hey there," the familiar British voice called.

He turned to meet Nina's sultry gaze. If she was trying to appear sexy, she was trying too hard. The halter-top was cut low while the skin tight skirt was cut thigh-high. Platform sandals added to her height and lengthened her taut bare legs. Her blonde hair was straight, cascading over her bare shoulders as it framed her dramatically made-up face and ruby lips. She was living up to the name, "Siren."

"Hi," he greeted, forcing a smile. "You look incredible."

"Thanks." She approached him, slipping an arm through his. "Shall we?"

They dined off the grounds at *La Fleur*, an intimate French restaurant in Mayville. Dinner was quiet with more staring on her part than actual conversation. For that, he was grateful. Having to make small talk with her wouldn't have been easy. After, they strolled the grounds from the gate to the inn. The sounds of woodwinds and orchestra from amphitheater filled the crisp night air.

"We can stop by and attend the Symphony," he said, trying to delay the inevitable.

"I have a better idea. How about a vintage bottle of Merlot in my garret?" she purred.

"Are you sure?"

"I've never been so sure about anything." She said, her eyes glittering.

Or anyone, he thought. Her mistake.

She gripped his arm as they walked up the front steps and into the inn's lobby. It was quiet and empty. The guests were probably at the Symphony, a good sign. She pulled away and led him upstairs. Her hips swayed as she ascended the three flights. Minutes seemed like an eternity as his mind was racing with thoughts of how to proceed. With caution.

Nina opened the door to her isolated corner room and flipped on the overhead light, its subtle low wattage giving the room a warm amber glow. A hint of lavender permeated the air. The space was small with angular dormers and ceilings. Chintz wallpaper, frilly curtains, doilies, and a pieced country quilt on the bed lent it an overly feminine touch. For some reason it didn't suit Nina. He thought her more the contemporary steel and glass woman.

She pointed to a lumpy wingback chair and he sat. He watched her sashay to a counter that housed a microwave and mini-refrigerator. She used a corkscrew to decant a bottle of red wine. After, she appeared with two filled wine glasses. She handed one to him.

"A toast?" she asked with a grin, clicking her glass to his.

He made a point of sloshing some wine on his hand. "Damn."

"Oh, my." She ran to the sink to get a napkin.

Quickly he removed a test strip, dipped into the liquid. The strip revealed that the wine had indeed been spiked with Rohypnol, the date rape drug." He stashed the strip in his pants' pocket.

When she returned, he quipped, "Great wine."

"I'm glad you approve." She sat across from him on the edge of an armchair, her skirt hiking up to reveal more of her thighs.

She was staring, probably wondering when the drug would take effect. He tried to determine what her next step would have been had he succumbed.

"The nomad in me is saying that it's time to move on," she said. "I'm growing tired of the solitude of this place. I could really use some action. My plan is to leave here and fly out to Vegas. A little gambling and debauchery is in order."

"Sounds like a plan."

"I really thought that you would be going with me." She sighed.

"Why would you think that?"

She shrugged. "I thought that we could just run off together and start over, but I see how that isn't possible."

"Why?"

He faked a yawn and she took notice.

"I thought you were different, but you are really no better than any other man." She shrugged. "I used my heart instead of my brain, and this is where it got me."

"Excuse me?" He forced another yawn.

"Actually, you are far more dangerous than other men."

"Why?" He tensed.

She stood before him. "I know who and what you are, Darrin Franklin Carter."

He jumped up from his seat, stunned.

She laughed. "I had to learn more about you and I learned too much. I saw the bi-fold in your room, your gun and some of your paperwork. I saw my name on your laptop How dare you implicate me."

"You broke into my room?"

"While you were sleeping. I just couldn't hurt you. I felt so betrayed. You lied about who and what you were," she said, an icy glare in her eyes. "My visit to the Institution was personal this time. I came to find a mate, since I'm getting older and really don't want to be alone. You were different, not old and not lonely. I thought that we made an agreeable couple. What a disappointment."

"Did you kill those men, Nina?"

"I found out about this place through David Morrow, and found out that his summer home had been turned into an inn. So, your parents owned the inn where that bastard David Morrow died? I'm glad because you betrayed me, thanks to that damn Troy Adams recognizing me. The one time I used my real name. I took a risk and everything went wrong. I was too upset to even think straight." She shook her head and glanced up at the wall clock. "I'm thinking straight now."

"So am I." He stepped in front of her. "Maybe some wine will calm you?"

She peered at her glass with apprehension and at him.

"Here, why don't you drink my wine, too?"

Her eyes grew wide.

"Nina, I did not drink your drugged wine. I'm not going to pass out. Don't get your hopes up."

She stepped back, hands to her face.

"Nina, why did you harm those men?"

She just stared, eyes growing larger and burning with fire.

"Why did you kill them?"

"I hate men. All of you are like my father and David Morrow. You lie and cheat and take advantage. You can't just have one woman. My father had to have every woman he met, and he passed me on to his friends like that lecherous Morrow. Bastard took my virginity. He hurt me. Men are just selfish users. Men don't know how to be kind or how to love. Not even you. I thought you were different, but even you are after the hired help. What do you find so alluring about that damn desk clerk? You don't know who to love, what love is. or how to love. I hate you! You all deserve to die!" She threw the glass of wine at him, the liquid dripping down his face and the front of his shirt and jacket. The glass crashed to the floor into jagged shards.

She rushed toward him with her hands out.

He moved out of the way before she could push him.

"You wanted to ruin my life but you did worse, you broke my heart!"

She stood across from him like an enraged lioness.

"You're going to die just like David Morrow. Burn in hell. Both of you!"

Before he could react, she reached over to the counter and removed a can. "Burn!"

Unscrewing the cap she doused liquid on the floor furniture and draperies before throwing the remaining liquid and the can at him. The pungent scent of kerosene mingled with the tart wine filled his nostrils.

"Your parents' inn burned down and they were incinerated. You'll meet the same fate." She struck a match, the orange flame flickering.

"Don't." He ran toward her, tearing off his damp, smelly sports coat.

She laughed and tossed the match on the chair. It ignited instantly, bursting into an orange fireball, as the flames traveled the kerosene trail. As the room erupted, Nina ran toward the door. Darrin chased after her, preventing her from opening it and escaping. Her plans were not going to work this time.

"Let me go!"

Her eyes were large, the flames flickering in them along with fear. She was screaming and kicking as he held her arms behind her back, immobilizing her.

"Don't all witches burn?"

At that moment, the building's smoke and fire alarms went off. Water from overhead sprinklers showered down on them, extinguishing the flames. The acrid smoke of smoldering fire was choking. Flashes of a fire so long ago appeared in Darrin's mind. For a moment he was back at the Carter Inn, fighting flames and saving Katy. He looked at the women he held and she was as far from being Katy. The squirming, crying, wailing woman was a cold-blooded murderer. What she had in physical beauty, she lacked in heart and soul. He could hear the sirens summoning the volunteer fire department echoing on the grounds. Soon, the police and sheriff's department would follow.

In the meantime, he would hold and guard her.

"Come on," he ordered, pulling her up. "If you don't stand, I will drag you."

"I'm ruined! Ruined!"

She looked up at him, the dampness of her tears and the sprinkler water causing her mascara and eyeliner to smudge into raccoon eyes. Choking back, she rose to her feet as he had her arms immobilized. She tried to kick him. He stepped on her instep. She squealed.

"Walk," he ordered, leading her out of the room.

He stopped, grabbed his pair of handcuffs with one hand and clasped her wrists tightly behind her back, pushing her against the hallway wall.

"Ouch! You're hurting me."

"Really? Imagine that?" He stood to face her. "How do you think your victims felt? Their families?"

"They were all old worthless men with one foot in the grave anyway. Just like my father, a no good son of a bitch and they were no different." She was still defiant.

"Why do you hate your father so much that you killed other men?" he asked, seeking answers.

She hesitated before speaking. "My father wanted my mother dead, so that he could inherit her fortune and live the lifestyle he felt entitled to. He spent his entire inheritance, and even his home was at risk. My mother had the money he lusted after. He provoked her horse. It was proven. My mother didn't die as he had planned but was left an invalid. She was trapped in a worthless body. I loved her and took care of her. When she did die, he celebrated instead of mourned. I hate him and his kind. So, I killed him. It was so easy to just inject him with Risperine. Everyone thought he died of a heart attack." She cracked a smile. "It was so easy … so easy …"

"Easy enough for you to kill innocent men?"

"Men are not innocent. You should know."

"I don't know."

"I loved to watch them die. When they took their last breath, I felt so alive." She sighed and cracked a revolting smile. "I felt so alive."

He heard fire, police and EMS race inside and up the stairs, heavy footsteps pounding the floors. The police chief and county sheriff called out for him.

"Here," he yelled, and turning to Nina, "The party's over."

When Katherine returned to the inn, her heart leapt from her chest. It looked as if the entire Chautauqua Police Department, Chautauqua and Mayville Fire Departments, EMS and the County Sheriff's Department had descended on her property. Gawkers meandered around in animated conversations. The scene was chaos and mass confusion. Panic gripped at her chest and it tightened. Her mind raced when she saw the crowd and law enforcement swarming like bees on a hive, and she expected the worst. What happened between Darrin and Nina? Was he another victim? She had to force her way into the front door. A fear of the unknown made her heart skip.

The rare time she left her front counter, something went wrong. She had decided to take a walk to get her mind off of Darrin and his tryst with Nina. The music of Beethoven lured her into the amphitheater. She sat and the Symphony drew her in and kept her. It was Darrin's fault that she wasn't there to protect her investment. If she lost the inn, she lost everything.

A uniformed officer securing the front door stopped her, and she told him who she was, begging for entry and he reluctantly allowed her.

The scent of burned wood and fabric irritated her nose, an oddly familiar scent that made her stomach churn. The scent burned her heart to the depths of her soul. Memories flooded her mind. *Not again!* She surveyed the lobby. Nothing appeared damaged on the first floor. Her front counter and the furnishings appeared to be as she left them.

Only the noise, shouting voices, and the acrid scent were overwhelming. Activity and pounding footsteps echoed down from the upstairs. The inn was taken over by law enforcement and fire personnel. She wondered what had transpired, and if Nina Wailson was the cause. Memories of another inn, of fire and smoke, law enforcement, and Darrin flashed in her mind. The thumping of her heart and the fear she had that night returned. Her head was spinning. Bile crept up in her throat and nausea set in.

"Katy." Darrin's voice cleared her befuddled mind. She looked up to see him descending the stairs. As he came close, the scent of turpentine lingered on him like stale perfume, while his shirt was stained with red wine. He was disheveled and concern wrinkled his brow.

He pushed his hair back with splayed fingers. Soon, he was holding her in his arms. She relished the intimacy and concern. His deep green eyes met hers and his emotions mingled with hers. They were teens once more, survivors of the fire.

"Nina?" she asked, snapping back to reality.

He nodded. "She's in custody with the Sheriff's Department."

"You caught your suspect?" A strange sense of relief washed over her, yet concern over her inn, and she trembled. "It smells like a fire."

"Nina tried, but your sprinkler system extinguished the flames before they could cause major damage. However, I'm afraid that your third floor garret is now in need of an overhaul. At least it's not the whole inn." He let out an audible sigh.

She knew that his mind was on another fire long ago.

"That sprinkler system cost an arm and a leg. I'm glad it worked."

"It was definitely worth it."

"But the whole place smells horribly. I can't imagine my guests wanting to stay here until it's aired out and cleaned up. I'll need to arrange other accommodations in the meantime."

"Always the innkeeper." A faint smile appeared on his tense face.

"What happens now?"

"Well, Nina gets to spend the night at the jail motel where she can check in but can't check out. Investigators are going over the crime scene, your garret, but should be gone soon. I get to fill out some paperwork and make some reports, but we finally get to relax."

"No rushing back to NYC?"

"Hell no. I already told my supervisor, and he agrees, that a couple of weeks here as a guest are well deserved."

"Okay, Brantley." She smiled, her mood lifting.

"Brantley is dead. You're stuck with Darrin."

"I prefer him anyway. I'm not into computer geeks."

Other innkeepers offered their services to aid with the clean-up so that she would be up and running the following week. Everyone understood the need for income, since they operated seasonally and on small margins.

The fact that Nina Wailson was a serial killer was not disclosed to the public. She was portrayed as a mentally unstable woman who was arrested for attempted arson. The Institution's fine reputation would not be tarnished. The Honeysuckle Inn, the recipient of some misfortune, would also keep its stellar image.

The management of the Athenaeum Hotel heard of her dilemma and offered her guests accommodations, allowing Katherine time to clean up the fire damage and refresh her inn. They had some rooms available and were gracious to let them to her guests at no additional charge.

Later that day, while Darrin was doing paperwork in his room, her guests packing and moving, she sat behind her lobby counter pondering the work to be done. The fire damage would have to be removed, drapes sent out for dry cleaning, floors scrubbed, rugs shampooed and laundry run. Water damage to the second floor ceilings would need to be addressed and repaired. A call was already made to the sprinkler company to reset the sprinklers. Her insurance company was contacted about her liability claims. Repairs to the third floor garret could wait until the end of the season. She didn't have the time or the inclination to tackle it. And Darren had spoken of relaxing.

He always seemed to appear when she was thinking about him. Carrying his nylon carry-on and computer bag, he emerged from the stairway and strolled over to her counter. He had changed into clean clothes.

"Okay, I'm ready to go and you're not even packed yet," He said, setting down his bags.

She looked up. "Excuse me?"

"You surely aren't spending the night here."

Was he serious? "Of course, I am. It's my inn."

"The place reeks. Even you need to get out of here after what transpired. Give it a break."

"But it's my inn, my home." Didn't he understand? His parents were innkeepers.

"This isn't a ship and you aren't the captain. Now, go to your apartment and pack an overnight bag. A beautiful suite at the Athenaeum awaits."

"You're serious?"

He grinned. Those dimples got her every time.

"I reserved the Presidential Suite. It's the least I can do for making your life hell ever since I arrived in this lobby. You deserve to be treated like a lady, and not the chambermaid. There's also a table for two with our name on it at the Heirloom Restaurant for dinner tonight. Better pack a fancy dress and your pearls."

"I don't own pearls."

"That will have to change in the near future." He stroked his chin.

"What's gotten into you?"

"I just solved a major case, thanks to your father. By the way, I sprung him from Westfield and he's joining us for lunch tomorrow."

"You really have this planned."

"What do you think I've been doing holed up in my room? Just working on F.B.I. protocol bullshit."

"As for this Presidential Suite. Does it have a single or a double bed?" There seemed to be a motive behind all of his ideas. Was he seducing her?

"King size. Big enough for two." He winked.

She swallowed hard. This was getting interesting.

"Get away from that counter. It's time to be a part of life already instead of living through other people. Your guests are having their fun; isn't it about time you have your own? Besides, we have a great deal of catching up to do."

CHAPTER 27

The suite was lavish by Chautauqua standards with its unique antique Victorian settees, chairs, draperies, fixtures and history. President Bill Clinton resided in this particular suite for a week, treating it as the executive mansion, while preparing to debate Senator Robert Dole during the 1996 presidential election. A view of the lake could be seen from the windows.

Darrin carried her small overnight satchel with his carry-on and computer case as they entered the spacious suite. For all of her years on the grounds, Katherine had never seen a room at the Athenaeum. Though impressed, she smiled. The antiques she had inherited and furnished her inn were equally as elegant in design and quality. Darrin's clearing his throat brought her back to the reality that she was alone with him. The king sized bed beyond seemed a bit looming. The thought of she and Darrin in that bed made her flush and warm all over.

So much had transpired during the past few weeks, in her life and with Darrin that she shook her head in amazement.

"Remember when we were kids, we dreamed of this place?" he asked.

She met his sparkling gaze. "The staircase outside and the veranda. I believe this room was never mentioned."

"I'd say it was implied." He winked.

She swallowed hard. Was the room getting hot or was it her? As if the fire at the inn wasn't enough.

"Look." Darrin pointed to the antique bureau where a wrapped gift basket was set.

Through the clear film, a bottle of champagne, crystal flutes, cheese, crackers and fruit could be seen.

"Someone's generous," she said.

"I guess we should check it out." Darrin went to the bureau and untied the ribbon that held the film. He withdrew the bottle of champagne. "Moët."

"Impressive."

"Someone at the hotel likes you." He removed the two flutes.

"Or feels sorry for me." She stood watching him remove the cork with a pop and a fizz. He poured the bubbling liquid into the glasses, took one for himself and handed her the other.

"To us. The survivors," he said, clinking his glass to hers.

She sipped, the bubbles tickling her nose and throat. He watched her as he drank from his glass.

He removed the plate of cheese cubes and crackers and carried it to the cocktail table, setting down his glass. When he went back for the fruit tray, she sat on the settee.

He set down the fruit in front of her and sat next to her.

"This is a nice touch. I bet you haven't had a bite since breakfast either." He took some cheese on a cracker and handed it to her.

She nodded, taking the cheese cracker and eating it. She was famished.

They ate more cheese, crackers, and fruit and drank champagne.

"We'll have to save some room for dinner later," he said.

Her mind wasn't on dinner.

He draped an arm over her shoulders. "We've come a long way, through the years and during the past few weeks."

She contemplated him, the angles of his face, his glittering green eyes, and lush lips. Was he really that handsome? When did the scrawny little boy grow up into an athletically-built man?

Before she could think further, his arms encircled her, drawing her close into him. Those lush lips were on hers, soft to the touch and yet hard and unyielding. So hypnotizing that she blanked out, relishing the touch and taste. She answered his kisses with her own. The heat rose in her cheeks and throughout her body and she trembled. Never had kisses aroused her so. Her lips parted and she welcomed his tongue to swirl and mingle with hers. Lightheaded, his taste and touch were so comfortable and familiar, so welcome.

"Katy, I've always loved you," he whispered, taking a moment for a breath.

Those were the words she had fantasized about for years after they parted. The fantasies and dreams that one day he would come back into her life to continue the love story that had begun in their youth. The impossible had become real. She gripped his arms to make sure that he was really there, to be assured that it wasn't a figment of her overactive imagination.

At her touch, he kissed her again with more intensity, his hands reaching up and under her tee shirt. She jumped, startled as her bra was unhooked and he chuckled. His smooth hands lifted up her shirt.

"If you don't take it off, I'm ripping it off. If you like the shirt, remove it," he whispered.

She hesitated before lifting it over her head in one swift motion, tossing it to the floor. "Better?"

"Almost." He drew a deep breath, removing her bra with his gaze before he pulled the silky bra down her arms and off, tossing it to the floor. "Oh my, what have we here?"

He cocked an eyebrow, staring at her very firm, pert breasts and, she was certain, the long faded scar and shriveled skin that ran across her chest down to her stomach. She swallowed hard at having him see the remnants of damage from the fire in their youth.

"You're beautiful," he said, looking up at her with an intensity hotter than any flame.

Tears formed in the corners of her eyes. "I look awful."

"No, you earned those stripes. Katy, those are signs of survival." He leaned down and planted a trail of kisses down her scars from her breasts to her stomach.

He touched her in the most vulnerable of places. What she saw as ugly, he made beautiful. What she wanted to hide, he embraced. If this wasn't love, she wasn't sure what was.

He sat. She watched as he removed his polo shirt to reveal his taut bare chest and a trail of crumpled skin on his own chest, a bare spot where hair wouldn't grow.

She swallowed hard. He had his own scars. Of course, he would understand and accept hers.

"Other people have tattoos, we have our scars. They are signs of our strength," he said in a low, gentle voice.

She reached out, and traced the outline of the space on his chest and sniffled.

He drew her into his arms and held her, burying his head in her amber curls.

"Oh, Katy. Katy," he whispered. "Where has time gone?"

He released his hold on her and stood. Taking her hand, he led her toward the bed. Tossing the floral bedspread to the floor, he moved the blanket and sheets aside. He sat, pulling her next to him.

"Oh, Katy, Katy," he whispered, kissing her on the lips, her neck, and earlobes. She tingled and shivered as his tongue circled inside her ear.

He traced a line of kisses down the line of her jaw, his hands unsnapping the top of her khaki slacks and pulling down the zipper.

He stopped to gaze into her eyes. He reached down to remove her sandals, one at a time, planting kissed on the insteps. After, he slid her slacks down her legs and off. She cringed, crossing her legs to hide a scar that ran down her right thigh.

"Oh, Katy, Katy," he whispered, moving her leg and tracing the scar with kisses.

She watched him stand to unbuckle his chino slacks. He reached into a pocket and removed a foil packet and dropped it one the nightstand. Her heart raced as he undid the top button, unzipped them and dropped them to the floor. Swallowing hard, she saw the prominent bulge in his snug boxer briefs. He removed the shorts. Had it really been that long since she saw a man's erection? Her body reacted with moist heat.

He came to the bed, leaned over and slid the bikini pants down her legs and off leaving her totally bare. She spread her legs, vulnerable and yet, wanton.

Leaning over her, he perused her nakedness and smiled as if in approval.

"I want to kiss you, every inch of you," he murmured, lips meeting hers.

Kissing him was so natural. His lips belonged on hers, his tongue an extension of her being.

She tingled as he kissed her mouth, neck, breasts, and the rest of her body intimately. His tongue followed, licking and tasting her. Sensations of heat and power traveled from her mouth, to her breasts to down … there. Gasping breathless, she moaned as he awakened the nerve endings on her flesh like electrical currents were firing. Never had anyone touched her so, and had such an effect on her. He awakened a body gone dormant for so many years. She was coming alive as a sexual being, and as a woman.

He moved aside, releasing his hold on her to caress her breasts. Fingers rolled her nipples,followed by his lips to suck and arouse.

"I want to love you the way you deserve to be loved," he whispered.

She squirmed hot and wet from want as his lips and tongue traveled down her breasts to her stomach and … Lower. Memories of a dank attic room on a dusty mattress returned along with the same sensation of desire. She wanted him, all of him, inside, filling her.

He reached over to the nightstand, grabbing the foil pack. "Ever the Scout, be prepared."

He unrolled and slipped on the condom and moved on top of her. She placed her hand on his sheathed member as he helped guide that part of himself into her. She was tight, and for a moment she felt like that fifteen year-old virgin.

"It's been a long time." She wanted everything to be easy and perfect but it wasn't.

"We'll just take it slow and easy."

And he did. Slowly, he filled her and she liked the way their bodies merged. They melded as one instead of two beings. Waves of pleasure ebbed and flowed with each thrust. By instinct, she drew her legs around his waist. *Deeper. Deeper.* She closed her eyes to focus on the sweet tension that built into a crescendo. One more thrust and she erupted into a numbing climax, a release so potent that her body shivered. He softly moaned as he came.

He lifted himself off and looked down at her with his sweaty brow and disheveled hair. His eyes glittered and she couldn't imagine a man being more handsome.

"Did anyone ever tell you how sexy you are?" he asked.

"He just did."

He leaned down to plant a soft kiss on her lips, rolling to her side. He placed and arm around her and drew up the sheet. Soon, he fell into a deep slumber.

To love and be loved was more important than any material possession, even the inn.

CHAPTER 28

The next morning, they sat at a quiet table in the Heirloom at The Athenaeum. A young waiter had just left with their breakfast order. Katherine sat next to Darrin, Troy Adams across from them. A sense of calm settled over her after the events of the past weeks. For the first time in years, the desire to flee to her inn and sit behind the counter was nonexistent. Her desire to be alone was gone, and she cherished the sense of belonging she had with Darrin and Adams. With Darrin, she discovered what love was. With Adams, she had real family. She smiled with genuine happiness.

"You look in fine spirits this morning," Adams said, his gaze wavering from her to Darrin.

"The trauma is over." For her it was more than just recent events, but those of the past as well.

"Thank goodness. Good job, Darrin." Adams reached out to pat Darrin's shoulder. "I knew that girl was a problem."

"Without your insight and help, I wouldn't have had enough information to investigate her."

"And my near death experience at her hands?"

"I will admit that your encounter with Nina provided strong evidence."

"How are you feeling?" Katherine asked, thinking about the insulin and hospital stay.

"Fine as can be expected. I'm sure the food here is better than what they served in the clinic." Adams winked.

"Speaking of food. Did Nina ever confess to why she poisoned the s'mores? It's weird because she wasn't even a guest when it happened." Katherine had been perplexed.

"Nina confessed to a great deal," Darrin began. "Actually, she used the free Sunday admission at the Institution as a way to enter the grounds undetected, to snoop around, and make plans. She surveyed the grounds like a cat stalking prey."

"Why the Institution?"

"She hated David Morrow. I feel better saying this, knowing he was not your biological father. Wills pushed her on David and he raped her and abused her when she was a teen."

Katherine drew her hands to her face. "Oh, no. She had a reason for revenge."

Adams sat listening intently as Darrin explained the case.

"Revenge brought her to the grounds. She knew that David had a home on the grounds, and discovered it to be the Honeysuckle Inn."

"So, she hated it, too?"

"Yep. Thus, she sent poisoned s'mores."

"But they were addressed to you, as Brantley."

"Only because other baked goods were being sent to me. At the time, she assumed I was just another old man."

"Because of her father and David, she took revenge on lonely, old men?"

"She said that they made her feel cheap and used, and vowed never to be taken advantage of again. She set out to right the wrongs done to her. Using her medical background and the knowledge that the Institution was a dating site for the lonely, she did just that."

"But she wanted you?"

"For some reason, she liked me and set out to make me her prize. She had decided to give up her hobby of murder, and actually settle down. She figured she'd quit before she was detected. She did her own investigating, and discovered that I was undercover and actually pursuing her. That's when she planned to kill me, and burn down the inn. She thought I'd meet the same fate as David Morrow. Fooled her."

"I bet. Will she be put away now?" Katherine rubbed the chills racing down her arms.

"She's been arraigned for the murders, will go to trial and the prosecution will likely be seeking the death penalty." Darrin smiled.

"I don't know. I feel both happy and sad." Katherine thought of Nina's beauty, money and education, and how she had thrown it all away.

"That Nina was a piece of work." Adams shook his head. "A real nut case."

"You said that you, David and Wills all attended Yale. You knew Wills rather well. Weren't you aware of David and Nina?" Katherine asked, wheels turning in her head.

"Sadly, no. I knew them socially, but wasn't privy to their private lives and their secrets. It's too bad. Maybe I could have prevented the tragedy."

Breakfast arrived. A reflective silence permeated the table.

"Hi, there," a woman's high-pitched voice broke the quiet.

Mildred stood in a denim skirt, tie-dyed tee shirt with rainbow knee-highs in her Birkenstocks. She stood, gaze focused on Adams.

He looked up and smiled. "Millie."

Millie? Katherine noticed a sparkle in his eyes.

"Oh, we met at the Cinema last night and had a delightful chat over ice cream," Adams explained.

Mildred was glowing. "I just got a table and noticed you here." Mildred pointed to a small corner table.

"Would you mind if I joined Millie?" Adams asked, rising.

"Uh, not at all," Katherine mumbled.

"I'm sure you youngsters would prefer to dine alone anyway," Adams said, picking up his plate and cup of coffee.

Before moving, Mildred said. "Nice seeing you, Brantley. I'm glad that you found a nice young woman."

They left.

Katherine turned to Darrin. "What a strange turn of events."

"Nothing surprises me anymore." He chuckled. "Your dad may have limited time, but he's going to have fun with that woman."

"You should know." Katherine thought of how Mildred had pursued him.

"She's not my type. You are."

The way he looked into her eyes penetrated the depths of her being. He was a part of her physically, mentally, and spiritually. She liked the way he looked at her, treated her, talked to her, and loved her. She was mistaken in thinking that she didn't need anyone. The inn could not replace human contact. It was a mere physical place. Love was Darrin Carter.

After breakfast, he escorted her out of the Athenaeum. The walked out of the side door, under the burgundy canopy and strode up the curving drive, and up the hill toward Bestor Plaza.

"There's one more thing we have to do to get rid of the past once and for all," Darrin said in a serious tone.

Her heart fluttered. "The Carter Inn? No!" She stopped in her tracks.

He took her arm. "We have to. Consider it therapy."

She swallowed hard.

"Trust me, this is as difficult for me as it is for you," he said. She knew that it was.

In all of the years that she resided on the Institution's grounds, she could not walk down the street where The Carter Inn stood. Better to avoid the past than to relive it. Darrin was opening up old wounds that she preferred be stitched up forever.

He took her by the arm and led her up the hill, turning on a street that seemed so familiar and yet so different. The same sturdy oaks towered overhead, the gardens colorful and scented. She looked about and realized that the grand Victorian with its gingerbread trim, turret, and multi-level porches was gone. Nothing stood to remind her of its glory and its tragic demise.

"There," Darrin said, pointing to a lot on which a small condominium complex stood.

Designed to look old, it resembled the surrounding architecture, blending in as if had stood for a century. The clapboards were painted a pale mauve, the gingerbread trim ivory. Baskets overflowing with New Zealand impatiens added color while hummingbirds fluttered about. A wraparound porch with wood rails surrounded the structure, white wicker furniture adding ambiance. A children's tricycle lay overturned in the small grass yard, a fairy garden added whimsy, and an herb garden with basil and thyme perfumed the air.

Katherine blinked. "Is this really where it stood?"

"Oh, yes." He looked up at the structure as if he were really seeing what had been instead of what was.

He grasped her in a tight hug. "I thought that I'd be melancholy, but actually I feel rather good. This building is so pretty and is filled with life. It's like a phoenix rising from the ashes."

She had to agree. After all, she had to overcome ghosts of the past when converting her home into an inn. Life went on, and there was nothing one could do about it. Progress. Change.

"Feel better?" she asked.

"Actually, yes. It's rather therapeutic. To think I was afraid of a street and a plot of land? There are more serious things to be concerned about." He released her and stood at her side, grasping her hand.

"Like murderers?"

"Yes. In my line of work, one's priorities change." He met her gaze. "Returning here made me realize how far I've come and where I need to be."

"Where do you need to be?" she asked, pondering about his eventual return to his life in NYC.

He met her gaze. "I need to be with you. I am in love with you."

She swallowed hard. The only man she was ever in love with admitted to still loving her.

"Let's enjoy these vacation days to catch up. Though I do have a life in the city, I plan on spending my free time here with you. And, I'd like to host you and show you the city that never sleeps. I may not have Brantley Wentworth's wealth, but my future is with you."

She had fantasized about him and their having a future together. Never in a million years did she think if would actually happen. So many years had passed before their paths crossed. At least they crossed.

"I don't care about Brantley's wealth. Actually, I don't require his money."

"You are so proud and self-sufficient. You know that I'll help you and the inn financially."

"Darrin, there is no need. When Troy Adams realized that I was his daughter, he began to make provisions for me in his estate plan. When he passes, I will be his sole heir. Actually, I'll have more funds than Aunt Agatha." That thought alone made her smile.

"You will be a force to be reckoned with. Will you still want me?"

"Of course. I'm in love with you, Darrin."

He squeezed her hand.

"It's just so sad that Troy is going to die, just when he entered my life."

"At least he entered your life and you get to spend some time with him. Better than never knowing."

"True." These next couple of weeks, she decided would be spent catching up with Troy Adams and Darrin. No more hiding behind the counter of her inn, hiding in the past. No more fearing the future. The past was over and done. The future was hers. For the first time in years, she was free,

"By the way, do you still dream of getting married on the staircase landing at the Athenaeum?" he asked.

"Only if you're the groom."

"That sounds like a proposal to me." He chuckled.

"No, only when you get on bended knee to ask."

"Okay. I see that an engagement is in our future.

Our future.

She liked the sound of it.

ABOUT THE AUTHOR

Purveyor of the written word, Nancy Loyan Schuemann has been writing since elementary school. Nancy is the author of *Cleveland, Ohio: A Photographic Portrait* and *On the Threshold of a New Century: The City of South Euclid, 1967-1999.* Her first novel was *Paradise Found.* She is the author of *Lab Test, Hearts of Steel, Wishes and Tears, The Right Combination and Special Angel*. With her newest novels, *Champagne for Breakfast* and *A Kiss in the Rain,* she is entering the realm of self-publishing.

She holds a BSBA in marketing from John Carroll University and has a background in sales, marketing and public relations.

Her website is: **www.NLSScribe.com**

Made in United States
Cleveland, OH
28 April 2026